MONSTER

CHILD

Also by Rahela Nayebzadah

Jeegareh Ma

Rahela Nayebzadah

MONSTER

CHILD

a novel

A BUCKRIDER BOOK

Buckrider Books is an imprint of Wolsak and Wynn Publishers.

Editor: Paul Vermeersch | Copy editor: Ashley Hisson | Dari copy editor: Hamed Rouzbehani
Cover design: Michel Vrana | Interior design: Jennifer Rawlinson
Cover image: Children visiting spring lambs on the farm, Victorian 19th Century © duncan1890, iStock; Abstract red watercolor background © carduus, iStock
Author photograph: Joseph Reeves
Typeset in Nassim Arabic, Haettenschweiler and Aktiv Grotesk Arbc
Printed by Brant Service Press Ltd., Brantford, Canada

Printed on certified 100% post-consumer Rolland Enviro Paper.

"La Ruelle Monstre" © Paul Matthew St. Pierre, 2019. Reproduced with permission.

10 9 8 7 6 5 4 3 2 1

The publisher gratefully acknowledges the support of the Ontario Arts Council, the Canada Council for the Arts and the Government of Canada.

Buckrider Books
280 James Street North
Hamilton, ON
Canada L8R 2L3

Library and Archives Canada Cataloguing in Publication
Title: Monster child / Rahela Nayebzadah.
Names: Nayebzadah, Rahela, author.
Identifiers: Canadiana 20200410237 | ISBN 9781989496305 (softcover)
Subjects: LCGFT: Novels.
Classification: LCC PS8627.A94 M66 2021 | DDC C813/.6—dc23

For my beloved sons, Malek Forest and Matin River

In loving memory of Carl Leggo

La Ruelle Monstre
cons and pushers,
surge of races,
mixed, apart,
they seek
familiar faces
in the crowd,
in rows of slums,
among losers and bums,
frag
ments
of old world order,
dregs
of post-apocalyptic disorder,
an exercise in anarchy
and zero-degree
narration
drugs
skids
thugs
kids
in Monster Alley.

— Paul Matthew St. Pierre, "La Ruelle Monstre"

PART 1 – ب

BEH

CHAPTER

ONE

Friday, March 17, 2000

"You're a disease, Beh," I was occasionally told, meaning one of two things: I was contagious, contaminating others with abominable infections; or like a tree, I branched out and slowly grew on people. And though they called me a disease — especially after trying to seduce my English teacher, Mr. Harvey — my sister, Shabnam, is the monster child. She's the one who cries blood.

This morning, I'm woken up by Padar. "Get up. Farhad's waiting in the car," he says.

I look over my shoulder to catch a glimpse of the time. It's not even 5:00 a.m. The birds aren't even chirping yet. "Can we have breakfast first?"

"No."

Getting out of bed, I try to make as much noise as possible. If I have to wake up this early on a Pro-D Day to see animals slaughtered for Mâdar's mehmouni, then so does Shabnam. I lift my torso and legs up in the air and let them fall down, hard.

Shabnam is still sleeping. The walls could cave in and she'd still be out cold.

I wish I looked as serene when sleeping. Despite her bloody tears, Shabnam sleeps with a faint smile, mouth closed and her hair neatly in place. I, on the other hand, sleep with my head buried in my pillow, my hair dishevelled and my mouth wide open. Some mornings, I wake up with a stiff jaw.

I grab a sweater from Shabnam's dresser and head out, but first I make sure to kick the door, loud and clear, before dragging myself down the stairs.

Mâdar is on her knees, scrubbing the kitchen tiles. "Why isn't she up yet?" she asks Padar, upset that Shabnam isn't behind me.

"She was up all night studying," Padar says.

"I was up later. I even woke up with a headache. You don't see me in bed," Mâdar says.

Alif, however, is all set, ready to go. Dressed in a bandana, camouflage pants, vegan boots and a shoulder bag filled with pocket knives he purchased after becoming a butcher at Kâkâ Farhad's Bismillâh Halal Market, my twat of a brother makes it no secret that he looks forward to our monthly excursions.

"Hunter by day, butcher by night," he tells me.

"You look stupid!"

"Not as stupid as you," he says.

"Get moving," Padar says as a horn honks outside.

A rusty, blue car awaits us. Being the penny-pincher that he is, I wouldn't be surprised if Kâkâ Farhad drives that thing into the ground.

"You trying to wake up the entire neighbourhood?" Padar says to his brother. Padar slams the passenger door shut.

"Salâm to you too, Kareem," Kâkâ Farhad says. "It's not like you get along with any of your neighbours anyway."

All these years, I don't think I've ever seen the two have a civil conversation.

Our cousin Amir scoots to the middle of the back seat, leaving Alif and me no other choice but to sit on either side of him. Amir spills over from his own seat, spreading his legs wide open. His thigh touches mine and I feel like puking. I squish myself against the door.

Amir doesn't take after his padar. Amir is short and stocky, and his padar is tall and lean. Amir is lazy and eats more than he breathes. Kâkâ Farhad is one of the hardest-working men I've ever seen. Back in his prime, he was a well-known wrestler of pahlwâni in Kabul. To this day, his medals and awards are polished and displayed in his home. He was known for his impeccable balance and brute force. At the end of every match, his clothes were torn to pieces. Without question, women who came to see Kâkâ Farhad twist and turn his hips from side to side wished it were their shoulders being pinned to the ground.

But just because Kâkâ Farhad was handed the better frame and height, it didn't mean that the rest of him was better. His thinning hair is unkempt. He has a creased forehead and a weather-beaten face. His eyes are sunken and hidden under dark circles. Two flaring nostrils are apparent on his crooked nose. His teeth are yellow, chipped and crooked, and his thin lips are buried under his facial hair. And he always stinks of cigarettes.

The sun shines directly into my eyes. Driving to one of just two farms in all of British Columbia that practise the Islamic methods of slaughtering, one can imagine how daunting the essence of collective sweat can be, especially when Kâkâ Farhad refuses to roll down the windows.

The air in the car smells like morning breath and armpits. Amir, in particular, has a peculiar body odour. He smells like qorma sabzi. Not even the pine tree–shaped air freshener hanging from the rear-view mirror can fend off the smell.

I'm not the only one irritated by the silence. Kâkâ Farhad gives in and plays rowza. Luckily, I brought my Discman with me so I don't have to listen to a bunch of men who sound like cats in heat.

I slowly drift into sleep and Alif nudges me. "Nice try, I'm not letting you sleep your way outta this."

Finally, Kâkâ Farhad pulls into a parking lot at Mostafa's farm. It's a two-hour drive from our rundown neighbourhood of crooks, stoners and illegals. I step out of the car and catch a whiff of fresh air at last. The sun is still blazing hot. My throat is dry. I lick the roof of my mouth.

Mostafa, dressed like he's about to attend a golf tournament, steps out of his mansion. He greets Kâkâ Farhad but not Padar. "Salâm, biâdar jân. Why don't you come inside and join us for tea? My wife just finished baking naan." Because the other halal farm is located in all-white Fort Nelson, Mostafa knows he can get away with being a dick.

"Thank you, but we're pressed for time today," Kâkâ Farhad says.

"Everything is set up for you. Let me know if there's anything else I can do," Mostafa says.

Padar and Kâkâ Farhad go searching for the chunkiest animals to slaughter, while Alif, Amir and I stand still, like three sterile testicles.

Mostafa's farmland is green and spacious. Lazy cows chew grass all day long. They're secluded far away from the sheep and goats. I don't know why Padar chooses to bring me here. Sometimes, I wonder if he mistakes me for a boy.

I spot one sheep from far away. It reminds me of Lamb Chop from *Lamb Chop's Play-Along*. I've never found any animal attractive, but this particular sheep is an exception. It's white, fluffy and plump. Its pink ears hang perfectly down its face. The teenager side of me wants to pet it. Luckily, Kâkâ Farhad spots a sheep that's fluffier and plumper. Lamb Chop is off the hook, at least for now.

Holding the animal by its fore- and hind legs, Kâkâ Farhad places it down on its side. "Allâhu Akbar, Allâhu Akbar. Bismillâh Arrahmân arrahim," he repeats.

Padar pulls out his qibla compass and places it on the ground. "The qibla is that way," he says, pointing east. Aside from butchering an animal, my family also prays in this direction five times a day.

For a short period, the animal tries to escape. From afar, I can see a tear dribble down its face. Animals aren't as dumb as they look — at this moment, it becomes clear to them that they're drawing their last breaths, and they submit themselves.

Padar hands Kâkâ Farhad a bottle of water from Alif's bag. The thirsty animal takes its last few sips. Again, it tries to fight and then willingly submits. Padar holds the animal's hooves together as Kâkâ Farhad lifts its head. When he makes the niyyat to slaughter, he utters, "Bismillâh."

With a sharp knife, Kâkâ Farhad slits the throat.

The blood flowing out of the animal is tranquilizing. I imagine every tension in my body releasing itself into that stream of blood. Even though the eyes are still moving and there's slight movement in the feet, I find myself lost in the deep red colour, a fascination I developed thanks to Shabnam. The aura of blood is so overwhelming that I can almost taste it.

Padar is drenched in the animal's blood, too. While it is hung up to drain, Kâkâ Farhad wipes the blood from his forehead. He passes the ragged towel to Padar, who then wipes his scalp, neck and forehead. Watching them pass a wet towel back and forth is more nauseating than watching the animal being cut open.

Padar unfolds a newspaper and places it on the prep table, then Kâkâ Farhad takes the animal by the legs and places it on the paper. There's something strange about butchering an animal that brings them closer. The younger brother does the dirty work, and the older does the bitch work. Whether Padar likes this is another story.

"My hands are bloody," Kâkâ Farhad tells Amir. "Go grab my bag of knives from the car."

Amir runs to the car, panting so loudly that even the animals can hear him. "I can't find it!" he shouts.

"You're just as useless as Mostafa's knives," Kâkâ Farhad shouts back. "Check the glove compartment!"

Overworked from the jog to the car, Amir decides to walk back, slowly, with the knives.

"Run! Astaghferullâh!" Kâkâ Farhad says. When disappointed by their children, white parents say, "Jesus Christ." Muslim parents, on the other hand, say, "Astaghferullâh."

Kâkâ Farhad pulls out his knives and places them neatly on the ground, from biggest to smallest. His knives are so sharp, you can lose a finger just by staring at them for too long.

Cutting through the wool is always the toughest task. Regardless of how sharp the knife is the outer coat doesn't peel off easily. After the rib cage is cut open and the internal organs are removed, the animal is chopped and layers of fat are trimmed. Finally, the animal is put into oversized garbage bags before it's transferred to a wheelbarrow and jammed into the trunk of the car. No part of the animal goes to waste in our household.

Slaughtering an animal according to Islamic practice is arduous. "Islam is the only religion that provides detailed responses to every matter pertaining to man's life," Mâdar would always say. There was no disputing, for even something as banal as slaughtering was thoroughly laid out, step by step, in Ayatollah Sistani's exhaustive text *Towzih ul Massâel*. Get even one step wrong and you'll be left with a harâm carcass.

First, the animal must be alive and fully capable of running away before it's slaughtered. And it's important that the animal is given a drink of water to show respect for both the animal and its Creator. Second, the slaughtering process is to be fast and efficient, so that the animal doesn't endure a long and painful death.

The incision, which occurs only on the throat, must be made with a sharp blade that can easily cut through the carotid artery. But right as the blade sits on the animal's throat, the phrase *Bismillâh* must be said, which is the third step. It's this utterance that separates halal meat from what Mâdar calls "Jewish meat."

Why does a thirteen-year-old know so much about slaughtering an animal? The answer is simple. I was born into an obedient Muslim family, which means that the moment our bodies can digest solid food, we're lectured on what makes an animal harâm and halal, a topic that isn't always black and white. In my diligent and overcautious family, everything has to be purchased from halal meat shops.

"Sunnis take everything so lightly. I've seen a few whisper 'Bismillâh' under their breath before eating the meat that's purchased from sinful grocery stores," Mâdar would always say. Being Shia meant being stricter, which is more favourable to my odd mâdar.

Then, there's one animal that's harâm at all cost. This animal is the pig, which I've always dreamt of eating. The smell of bacon is my nemesis.

"Since we're here, I can use one sheep for my shop," Kâkâ Farhad says.

"Then let's hurry. Like you said, we're pressed for time today," Padar says.

*

Unfortunately, I didn't see which sheep they killed. I was in the car, passed out from fatigue and hunger. It could've been Mr. Chop, but I was too tired to give a shit.

Again, Alif nudges me. "Wake up, sleepyhead," he laughs.

"Shut up, I'm fucking tired."

"Stop with those awful English swear swords," Padar says. He looks over at Kâkâ Farhad and says, "The great English language has only provided these children with a list of foul swear words."

The drive home is unbearable as I'm overtaken by hunger. My stomach growls, demanding to be fed. "Can we stop somewhere to eat?" I look over at Amir, hoping that he'll join me in my whining, but he's too busy picking his nose.

"No, we'll be home soon," Padar says.

We come home to the smell of spices and household cleaners. I inhale deeply.

Everywhere is tidy, not a speck of dust anywhere. Our home looks better now than it did when we first moved in — at least on the inside. It used to be a grow op, like a lot of the homes in our end of Vancouver.

"Why are you wearing my sweater?" Shabnam asks. "If those bloodstains don't come off, you're buying me a new one."

"*You* are bothered by bloodstains?" I ask.

From the moment Shabnam was born, people thought she was a monster for crying blood.

I walk to the stove, but before I can catch a glimpse of what's cooking, Mâdar stops me. "I'm hungry," I say.

"Don't you dare. That's all for tonight. Go wash up. You reek of animal guts," she says.

Mâdar's a great cook. There's no secret ingredient to her finest dishes, all of her masterpieces consist of the same herbs and vegetables. Olive oil, minced onions, crushed garlic, diced tomatoes and chopped cilantro come together to create rich flavours.

The fragrance of fresh-baked naan makes me drool. Mâdar slices it half an inch, according to her measuring technique. She spreads out her fingers, wide. From the tip of her thumb to the tip of her pinky, Mâdar considers that to be half a foot. I wait for her to look away before I sneak a piece in my mouth.

"You're a disease," she tells me. "Didn't I tell you to stay away from the food?"

Whenever we host any mehmouni, we're not to come anywhere near the food. Even more, we're not allowed to help ourselves to any food in the fridge because Mâdar throws a fit about the pile of dishes she'll be stuck washing all day.

Mâdar is cooking her favourite stew, kala pâcheh. Her version, however, is more elaborate, for it includes tongue, eyes, heart, legs and tripe. "We cook it differently than the Iranians. They only use the head and the hooves," she'd brag, as she often does with most of her dishes.

Before Padar and Alif even get the chance to place the meat on the kitchen countertop, Mâdar reveals her frustration toward her husband.

"What took so long? How'd you expect the kala pâcheh to be ready by six?" she asks him.

"You can ask Farhad when you see him tonight," Padar says in his defence. "And don't worry about time. Farhad already told me that Amir plans to lead prayers first, so that'll buy you some more time."

I'm already swearing under my breath. Maghrib isn't until 7:30 p.m. Then guests will need half an hour to settle in, mingle and what not. Mâdar and the other ladies will easily take up another half an hour in the kitchen, reheating and serving the food. Plus, being the hosts, we'll have the privilege of eating last — always the selfish men are served first, then the reserved women and then the starving children. I'd be lucky if I had anything to eat by 9:00 p.m.

"Still, it needs to cook for at least eight hours," Mâdar replies. "Now all three of you, get out of my kitchen and clean yourselves. It's not like I wasn't up early scrubbing every wall in this house. There's now an ache in my back because of it."

"You weren't alone, Mâdar," Shabnam says.

"Quiet. You showed up when most of the cleaning was done," she says.

"It'll be fine," Padar interrupts. "Tomorrow's a weekend, Farzana. You can keep your guests for as long as you please."

"I better not catch you sitting in front of the television watching *Rambo* or *Terminator* all day," Mâdar says.

"I was actually thinking of washing the car," Padar says.

Mâdar rolls her eyes. "The meat must be separated into bags and put in the freezer first," she says.

Padar ignores Mâdar's demand. "This is all going to go to waste. There doesn't need to be meat in every single dish."

"None of this'll go to waste. It's better to have leftovers than to have our gossipy guests from mosque go home hungry. If you're going to throw a nazr at your home, Kareem ăqâ, then it has to be done right. Our aberou is on the line," she says. Aberou means a lot to the both of them, except when it comes to expensive dinners, then aberou takes a back seat for Padar. "You want people to say that Kareem khân has enough money to open up a restaurant, but not enough to feed a few mouths?"

Mâdar's annoyed, we know this because she uses honorifics sarcastically.

Mâdar and Padar never work as a team. Every mehmouni looks the same: Mâdar, the stress case, unnecessarily tires herself out, slaving for days; while Padar, the sits-on-his-ass husband, tries getting out of any kind of work by busying himself with random errands.

Padar runs upstairs to shower while Alif sneaks out to the backyard to busy himself with friends. But just as I'm about to leave, Shabnam complains. "Hurry up, there's a lot to do in the kitchen," she says, sounding a lot like Mâdar.

I stick my tongue out at her. "I already did my part."

"Why don't I ever get to go to the farm?" Shabnam asks Mâdar.

"Let's see how you handle sheep head in a pot of boiling water first," Mâdar says.

Upstairs, I take Shabnam's sweater off and throw it on her bed. The air is suffocating. Mental institutions look more inviting than our room. Mâdar has "tidied" it, which means she's taken down all of my love poems and sketches of Mr. Harvey and hidden them under my bed, like she does whenever we have company. Now, our room is no different from the other rooms in the house. Aside from the nazars and the praying timetable, all walls are bare.

I open the window to let the stink of toxic chemicals out. Alif is still in the backyard, playing marbles with Ryan and Terry, freckle-faced twin brothers who live across the street. With their greasy complexions and freckles splattered all over their faces, they look like pepperoni cheese pizzas.

With a wooden stick, Alif traces a circle on the ground. "You go past this circle and you're out." He then digs a hole in the centre of the circle and says, "The rules are simple, whoever gets their marble in the circle wins and is the first to play the next game."

He looks over at Terry, wanting to weed out the weak. "You go first," Alif says. Terry shoots his marble too fast, which rolls out of the circle.

"You're next," Alif tells Ryan. Ryan shoots his marble too slow, which stops a few inches away from the hole.

Finally, Alif shoots his marble. It lands right into the hole.

"Fuck that! You cheated," Terry says.

"Fuck you!" Alif says. "You wanna cry like a little bitch then take your marble and fuck off."

Alif takes more marbles out of his tin can, which he keeps buried in the backyard close to the apple tree. In a straight line, he spaces out fifteen marbles. "Again, whoever goes past this circle is out," he says.

He takes his lucky marble out and shoots for the shiny blue marble in the middle. They take turns. If played with skilled players, the game can take up to hours, but because Alif is playing against a bunch of losers, it ends quickly. One by one, Alif shoots his marbles out of the circle.

"I won. I get to keep your marbles," Alif says.

"What do you mean *you* get to keep them?" Ryan asks.

"I shot all fifteen out of the circle so they're mine."

"Go fuck yourself. You only keep the marbles you shoot out of the circle," Ryan says.

"You don't even know how to play," Terry adds. When he gets mad he looks constipated.

"You both go fuck yourselves. I was playing marbles in my mother's stomach, way before you were a fucking sperm in your daddy's balls," Alif says.

"This isn't Afghanistan, that's not how we play it here," Terry replies.

"My marbles, my rules," Alif says.

A laugh from next door diverts Alif's attention. The laugh is coming from Jonathan, Alif's archenemy. Jonathan scrunches his face, looking like a yeast infection.

"What you laughing at?" Alif yells.

Jonathan is always sitting on the back porch step, staring off into the distance. It's been years since he's moved next door into Mr. and Mrs. O'Connors' foster home, and no one has heard him say one single word. Some say his parents traded him for a can of beer and that he's a result of booze and prescribed drugs. Others say he was dropped on the head way too many times as a child. I say he ran away from juvie. I bet his real name isn't even Jonathan.

"You deaf? What you laughing at?" Alif yells.

Again, no answer.

"That's what I thought." Just as Alif is about to pocket Ryan's and Terry's marbles, Mâdar catches him. He hurriedly puts the marbles in his pocket anyway.

Mâdar, with Shabnam slowly walking behind her, brings a large plastic container filled with animal parts and places it down on the yellow, trimmed grass. She's hard as nails. Her arms are designed for this, for she's done it countless times before.

Suddenly, straight out of an animal rights horror film, a sheep head falls out and lands right in front of Shabnam's feet.

Mâdar picks the head up and throws it in the air before catching it. Jokingly, she says, "In Afghanistan, we'd use the head of animals to play marbles. Want to give it a try?"

Terry's and Ryan's jaws drop. They run off in fear. Mâdar lets out a laugh as Alif covers his face from humiliation.

"Put the tushlas away or I'll call your padar," Mâdar demands. "Bacha hâye bâzingar play tushla." Bacha hâye bâzingar are child-molesting men that force young boys to dance for their pleasure.

Shabnam rolls her eyes at Mâdar.

Again, Jonathan laughs. He heads inside as he sees Alif rush over to the fence. Lucky for him, Mâdar stops Alif. "Go pick some apples from the tree," she says. Then, pointing to the sheep's head, she tells Shabnam, "Pick it up."

Shabnam doesn't respond.

"You're going to have to touch it sometime."

Again, no response. She stares at the head, looking saddened by the fact that it once belonged to a living creature.

Mâdar places the head back into the container and says, "You're useless! When I was your age —" She stops herself because she knows we've heard about her past so many times that we've all become numb to it. Instead, she says, "And here you were upset that you didn't get to go to the farm and Beh did."

Shabnam appears to grow light-headed, whether it's from the scorching sun or animal parts is a mystery.

Even though the trees and the leaves create shade, their skin is drying and cracking from the intense heat. Afghan parents rub crushed ginger on their children to prevent their skin from peeling away. Mâdar, however, persists in her dress. She wears a flower-patterned hijab and a long buttoned dress with loose-fitted pants underneath.

Mâdar lights the outdoor gas burner with a match. Shabnam breaks a sweat and boob sweat stains appear on her shirt. She takes it off, wearing only a tank top underneath.

"What do you think you're doing? Put your shirt back on," Mâdar says.

"I'm sweating. It's so —"

"I don't care — the flames in hell are far worse. How'd you think I feel? Cover up or go back inside and put something *less inviting* on."

"But Beh can flash her —" Shabnam tries to say.

"But she didn't! Besides, Beh's a runt. Her breasts haven't even developed yet. There's nothing to look at."

Alif jumps off the tree and comes running like he does whenever he sees fire. "Lemme try," he says. Alif is obsessed with fire, loving everything about it — the smell, the flickering and burning, and the vicious flames.

"Come any closer and it'll be you I'll be burning," Mâdar says. "I asked you to pick some apples."

"You're going to see how much work kala pâcheh requires. Still, be grateful you're in Canada. Children back home weren't so fortunate; kala pâcheh was for the rich," Mâdar tells Shabnam.

Mâdar grabs the head and slowly burns the hair off by placing it on the flame. She doesn't wear gloves or use tongs because she's a true Afghani woman. The foul scent of anything burning is one thing, but the stink of hair burning is another.

"Give me a hand. Grab one of the legs and start burning the hair off. You can't just stand around," Mâdar says.

Shabnam grabs a leg and watches each strand of hair sizzle. Mâdar smiles at her. "Make sure you get every strand. The last thing we'd want is to have guests find sheep hair in their food," she says.

Shabnam's hands begin to burn. She places the leg down as Mâdar grabs another. She rubs the hair on the leg against Shabnam's burning palm and says, "Keep rubbing. It'll help with the burning."

"It would be a lot quicker to do this over the stove, but the smoke detector will go off," Mâdar says, trying to make small talk. "That's how it's supposed to be done. Back home, the bone marrows would cook for hours on hours in a stove oven, leaving a syrupy broth. Nothing is healthier than the broth of kala pâcheh."

Smoke from the fire chokes the air, causing a blinding effect. Yet, even through the haziness, Shabnam's titty sweat is visible. Shabnam looks over the fence, probably hoping that the neighbours aren't home to criticize and mock Mâdar's strange practices. Luckily, Jonathan is still inside, not watching from his back porch step.

Mâdar turns the propane off and heads back to the kitchen. Shabnam willingly takes her lead.

I wash up and join Mâdar and Shabnam in the kitchen.

Mâdar scoops two cups of flour into a mixing bowl. She covers the sheep's head and legs with flour. Shabnam lets out a loud sneeze. "Now, we're going to have to scrub the animal clean. When you're burning the hair off, the legs and head turn black, which is what you don't want," Mâdar says, as she hands Shabnam a scrubby. Mâdar scrubs the head until it's white. "Think of the flour as bleach," she says. She's obsessed with bleach and whiteness. I'm surprised she didn't soak the animal in bleach.

Shabnam passes the legs to her so that she can scrub them a few more times. Next, Mâdar places a thick wooden cutting board on the kitchen countertop and grabs a leg, placing it on the board. With a sharp knife, she splits open the toes. "It's very important that the hooves are clean. All the lymph nodes must be removed," she says.

"From this point forward, the fun is over. Even I don't like this part," she says, now placing the head on the cutting board. She cuts off the ears and bangs the head hard against the countertop.

"What are you doing?" Shabnam asks, with a look of repulsion on her face.

"You're right. It's not going to work in here. Follow me," Mâdar says.

Once outside, Mâdar starts slamming the earless head on the patio out back. "What are you doing?" Shabnam asks again.

"I have to make sure that I get all the mucus out," Mâdar says.

Suddenly, Shabnam's breakfast makes its way up. Mâdar was right, the fun is over. She flips the head and, with her knife, cuts it open, beginning from slightly above the nose to the top of the forehead.

We head back to the kitchen, with the same look of disgust on Shabnam's face.

"Alif!" Mâdar yells. He runs down the stairs, always at her beck and call. "Grab me Padar's pliers and then hose out the patio for me."

"Yes, Mâdar," he says.

"What'd you need pliers for?" Shabnam asks.

"Wait and see," Mâdar says.

One by one, she yanks the teeth out of the head, heartlessly. I carefully inspect each tooth: some are big, some are stained and some look sharper than a blade. Mâdar then scrubs the gums and the top of the tongue until they are clean.

Then she transfers the head and legs into a large pot. Shabnam lets out a sigh of relief, but Mâdar grabs a spongy, wrinkly and dirty-looking sac from the bottom of the plastic container.

Before Shabnam opens her mouth, I ask, "What happened to the sheep's nuts? His sac is empty."

Another slap on the back of my hand.

"It's the shikamba, the tastiest part," Mâdar says.

I mistakenly think Mâdar is going to cut the tripe open violently, like she did with the ears and nose, but instead, she gently scrapes out the insides with a small kitchen knife. Suddenly, an overpowering stench takes over the house.

"I smell poo," Shabnam says.

Mâdar lets out a laugh. "It's everything that's been digested by the sheep. It's not even that bad. Imagine if that were you. It'd be a lot smellier."

Mâdar's cleaning is thorough. The tripe completely changes colour.

"Pay attention. When you go off to your husband's home and have guests over, you can both serve my recipe, even though I may not be around when that time comes," Mâdar says. She always likes to think of her death, which drives all of us insane. Some people like not knowing what tomorrow will bring, but Mâdar likes not knowing when death will pay her a visit. "Will you tell your guests you learned this recipe from your mâdar?" she asks.

"I'd have to be crazy to serve this to anybody," Shabnam says.

Mâdar happily shakes her head at Shabnam, knowing that her genetics aren't to blame for the way she is. Shabnam's birth mâdar died when giving birth to her. A few weeks later, Padar met Mâdar. "Marry me and be my child's mâdar," he said, an offer she couldn't refuse, especially since Shabnam was a green-eyed child that wept tears of blood. The two were wed on the war-torn fields of Kabul "with no ring in hand or a sekka to my name," as Mâdar put it, and entered Canada as refugees. Nine months later, she popped out Alif.

Mâdar loves all of us equally, even if she whispers the word *andar* behind Shabnam's back. Padar's the only one who's not tangled in this mess — all three of us are his biological children.

But whether he loves the child born to his first love more is something I think about.

Shabnam's birth mâdar also haunts my thoughts. Did she too have cursed green eyes? Was she beautiful, or big-boned like Shabnam? Her name cannot be mentioned out loud, for doing so will enrage Mâdar. "I can never seem to replace your Hazara wife," she'd say during every single argument.

The rest of the day runs smoothly, with plenty of food that isn't foreign to either of us.

"I'm only making one shank per person, so I have to make sure to tell this to Kareem ăqâ before he helps himself to more," Mâdar says. She takes a deep breath. "I have to make sure that there's enough food for everyone." Mâdar has poor judgment. No one can blame Padar for always being irritated with her.

Hours have gone by and the only dish remaining on the menu is haleem. Accustomed to heat, Mâdar sticks her hands in the pan and shreds the meat into small pieces before setting it aside on a dish (which she'll most likely complain about later for washing).

As the haleem slowly comes to a finish, Shabnam struggles to stand on her two feet.

"Kareem!" Mâdar yells. "Come taste the haleem."

Padar rushes into the kitchen. Mâdar and Padar are the only ones that eat the gluey mixture.

"Be careful, you'll dirty your white payran tomban," says Mâdar.

Alif enters thereafter.

"It needs more sugar and cinnamon," Padar says.

Suddenly, we're interrupted by the doorbell. I look over at Mâdar, who looks panicked and worried. "Who's that? It's only six thirty," she says to Padar.

"You did invite your guests for six," Padar says.

"I'm not even dressed. That must be Massud and his wife. They're always trying hard to appear Western by proving to others that they show up on time. Let them in. I'll be down in a bit," she says.

Hurrying to the stairs, Mâdar falls to the floor. We all rush to her aid.

"Are you okay?" Padar asks.

"I could've sworn I saw two stairs side by side. I'm so tired that I'm seeing double."

Padar stares at Mâdar and lets out a faint smile. "Everything looks great, Farzana. You've been working hard for days. Thank you."

The sternness on Mâdar's face fades as she smiles back at Padar. Me and Alif also smile as we watch them. A moment like this is not easy to capture.

Mâdar is right. Massud and his wife are the first to arrive. Massud smells of cheap hair gel and cologne, which makes him look like a rapist. His wife, whose name I've lost track of — from her Persian name, Rehaneh, she's changed her name back and forth to Rihanna, Renata, Renee, Rhea and Raina within the past few months — is dressed like a hooker.

I stare at her high heels as she hands her fur jacket to Alif. If Mâdar knew, she'd rip her a new one. Time and again, Mâdar reminds us that we're not to enter the house with our shoes on. "I pray on these floors," she'd say.

The couple have only been in Canada for two years and already they're unrecognizable "white Afghans" — a term Padar uses to refer to Afghan sellouts that trade their identities for Western ones. "People change when they come to Canada. They lose themselves," he'd always say. "The minute they can stand on their own two feet, they think they're better than everyone. When we first came to Canada, we mistook canned cat food as meat."

The first time we had them over for dinner, Massud's wife was covered from head to toe. Mâdar knew that in a matter of time she'd slip through the cracks. "With that amount of makeup, I don't see a reason to cover your hair," Mâdar whispered to Padar once, fully aware that he was checking her out. And, as Mâdar had anticipated, at the next dinner, she wore a sheer veil and let out a few strands of hair. By the third time, the veil was gone. Even their daughters, Sahar and Sara, have whitened — with blonde highlights and four piercings on each ear, they look like every other girl in school waiting to pop their cherries. No one in our community respects them — they only get invited to events because they donate to our money-hungry mosque, Ya Hosein Mosque.

It's obvious that Padar is attracted to whatever her name is. This one time, I heard him sing a perverted song about her when he was shaving his beard in the bathroom. "Mâdar, pray that I be kept alive for a long time only for Massud's wife, who has huge breasts that are shaped like plums," he'd sung.

"Where's your wife?" Massud's wife asks.

"She's upstairs, getting ready," Padar says, trying very hard not to look at her tits.

"I'm sorry," Massud says, "we didn't expect to arrive so early."

"There's no need to apologize. Others should arrive momentarily," Padar says, trying to appear proper. Alif prevents himself from laughing, knowing that Padar can never keep up with Massud's wealthy manners.

As Mâdar makes her way down the stairs, other guests arrive. Mâdar looks exquisite in her long dress and jewel-encrusted veil.

The entire mosque is over for dinner. Out of fear of Mâdar's wrath, Shabnam and I greet every woman by kissing them on both cheeks. For the elder women, we first kiss their hands and then their sweaty and prickly cheeks.

"Mubârak," the guests say, congratulating us on the opening of our family business.

Mâdar burns esfand to ward off the evil eye. The smoke detector goes off. "These Canadian smoke detectors are too weak. In Afghanistan, we didn't have to worry about this," she says, laughing.

"That's because smoke detectors don't exist in Afghanistan," Alif says, jokingly, to Amir. Mâdar looks at Alif with two darting eyes, enough to get him to stop giggling.

"May the evil eye be far. May our house always be filled with guests, inshâllah," Mâdar says.

I press my hands against my belly to prevent it from growling.

Casual conversation is put on hold as the azân from the gold-plated and Medina-shaped alarm clock goes off. It sends a faint chill down my spine. The clock never fails to remind us of our duty to kneel before Allah. Men and women line up to do their wudhu while Padar unravels the prayer mat and Mâdar reaches for her finest mohrs and tasbehs.

I don't like the way these boors perform wudhu; the bathroom counter is completely covered in water, forming large puddles right beneath my toes. Even the toilet seat is wet. I can't make out if it's urine, water from the watering can or a combination of both.

Mâdar can't keep her eyes off of Massud's wife. She's looking at her to see if she'll pray. "She didn't even line up to do her wudhu. I can even see her legs from here. Towba," Mâdar whispers to Khâla Wajma.

"You're being rude. What if she hears you?" Khâla Wajma says. She can get away with saying anything because she's a plump, jolly woman. But she's far more evil than the queen with the poisonous apple.

The room is quiet. Everyone waits for Amir to lead the prayer. He places his prayer cap on his head and brings his feet close together so that they touch. He looks down at his mohr before he lifts both hands up to his ears and says, loudly, "Allâhu Akbar."

During Namâz e Jamâ'at, men and women are permitted to pray together, except the women are to pray behind the men.

Amir clears his throat and recites the azân.

"Allâhu Akbar

"Ash-hadu an-la ilaha illa llah

"Ash-hadu an-la ilaha illa llah

"Ash-hadu anna Muħammadan-Rasulullah

"Ash-hadu anna Muħammadan-Rasulullah

"Ash-hadu anna Aliyan wali-ul-lah

"Ash-hadu anna Aliyan wali-ul-lah

"Hayya 'alas-salāh

"Hayya 'alas-salāh

"Hayya 'alal-falāh

"Hayya 'alal-falāh

"Hayya 'ala khayral amal

"Hayya 'ala khayral amal

"Allâhu Akbar

"Allâhu Akbar

"Lā ilāha illallāh."

In uniformity, Mâdar, Padar, my siblings and the guests — including Massud and his wife — rise, bow and kneel together. It's not long before I find myself annoyed by Amir's attempt to stress every vowel and accent in the prayers, especially when I know he doesn't sound like he's deep-throating when he's not leading prayers.

I cross my legs and twist and turn my hips to prevent myself from farting. No matter how hard I clench, a puff manages to escape. Even Alif is distracted. He tries to hold back his laughter as he steps on his neighbour's feet when getting in rokou' position. This continues until all prayers are complete.

Finally, the moment has arrived. Men fill their plates and eat in the living room, away from the women, who eat in the family room. Vibrant conversations occur among the men; silence among the women where the only noises heard are delicate chewing sounds and the occasional forks and spoons that hit the plates. The women play coy, they do not fill their plates or go for seconds. Mâdar has to constantly demonstrate her hospitality.

"Beh, pass Latifa jân the yakhni palaw," Mâdar says.

"Beh, pass Shokufa jân some of that mâhicha, why don't you?" Mâdar says.

"Shabnam, fill Kareema jân's plate with more haleem," Mâdar says.

Never would I be so stupid as to refer to these women as *jân*. They're all a bunch of phonies — put them in a room all alone and they'd be shoving food down their faces until it came shooting out of their assholes. Because of them, I can't even fill up my plate because Mâdar will accuse me of being unladylike.

Raucous banging noises are heard from the men. Pretending to go to the washroom, I poke my head in the living room. Padar is cracking the animal's head open with a hammer.

"The brain is my favourite part," Padar says. "When we were children, Padar would never let us try it. He'd lie to us, saying the brain would give us nightmares so that he could have it all to himself."

"He was lying to you," Kâkâ Farhad says. "He'd save the brain for me because I needed the extra fuel for pahlwâni. But I have to disagree with you. The eyeballs are the tastiest." He lifts up an eyeball and places it in his mouth.

Suddenly, I have no desire to eat anymore.

Alif, with a towel on his shoulder, comes around with a jug of warm water and a basin, so that the lazy men can wash their hands. This is also a signal for the women that dinner is over and domestic roles are to be filled.

The women tidy, while the men help themselves to cups of saffron-flavoured black tea, trail mix, elephant ear–shaped pastries sprinkled with icing sugar and pistachios, and apples.

"These apples are picked from our tree, please help yourselves," Mâdar says once the women finally join the men and sit across from them.

I want to join Alif and Amir in their game of Pogs, but Mâdar always warns me well in advance that I'm only to socialize with the girls during social functions.

Now that the men's and women's bellies are full, typical conversations follow.

"Our youngest daughter, Sahar, won a medal for having top marks in her grade and our eldest, Sara, won a plaque for having the best grades in the entire school," says Massud.

"My eldest is studying to become a doctor," Padar says.

"I am?" Shabnam says, confused.

Alif and I nearly choke from laughing too hard. In every gathering, parents brag about their children's fictitious successes. If one parent lies about their child studying to become a lawyer, another parent will lie about theirs studying to become a judge. If one says their child is a doctor, another will say that theirs is a surgeon. This can go on for hours.

"All this talk reminds me of one particular joke . . ." Padar says after being caught in a lie.

Go on, I think to myself.

"A daughter came up to her padar . . ." He pauses to make sure that everyone is paying attention. Once all eyes are on him, he continues.

I tune out. I've heard this joke at least a thousand times.

"She tells him, 'Padar, I wish to be an optometrist.' 'What's an optometrist?' her padar asks. 'An eye doctor,' she replies, with a big smile on her face, thinking that her padar would be proud. 'Daughter,' he says to her, 'a human has only two eyes. Study a profession that'll keep you busy and employed for a long while. Become a dentist,' he says. 'Why a dentist?' she asks. 'Because the average human being has thirty-two teeth,' he says."

Everyone chuckles. I convince myself that they're only doing this out of politeness.

Still trying very hard to keep his guests entertained, Padar decides to pick on Alif. "Padar nalât Canada. Put those Pogs away," he says.

In my community, the curse *padar nalât Canada* is used more frequently than *padar nalât*. Most Afghans in Vancouver, including my parents, dreamed about Canada, thinking money grew on trees here. "Free education, free medical and reasonable child tax benefits," they'd tell their friends back home. Years pass, and after discovering that nothing is handed on a silver platter, they begin to curse Canada and say, "We should've just stayed put and had families from Khârej send us money" or "Damn this kâfir country."

"Farhad, let's teach these boys how to play a real game," Padar says. He scans the room for Mâdar. "Farzana, boil a dozen eggs."

"What for?"

"For tokhm-jangi. We're going to teach the boys how to play," he says, courageously, knowing that Mâdar will comply in the presence of guests.

"Then what's the point of having the restaurant open on the first day of Moharram? You know better, Kareem ăqâ. It's harâm," Mâdar says.

"Nonsense! Back home there was no talk of this. The sheiks here will deem everything harâm, whether it be card games, tushla, chenâq or what have you."

I'm very drawn to this side of Padar. Alif and Amir lean in closer.

"If I may, what is the point of having your restaurant open on the first day of Moharram?" Massud's wife asks.

"It's because of Moharram, Islam exists . . . hijab exists," Mâdar says. Khâla Wajma nudges her.

Fifteen minutes later, Mâdar enters with a bowl containing a dozen hard-boiled eggs.

Padar hands half a dozen to his brother. The guests gather closer. Everyone, except for Mâdar, is excited for the game to begin.

"We each take turns to smash the opponent's egg without breaking our own. The player with the unbroken egg wins," Padar says. Both of their taps are light. After a few taps back and forth, Padar breaks his egg.

"Lemme try," Alif says. He shoves an egg into Amir's hand. With the first tap, his egg cracks.

"Gentle," Kâkâ Farhad says, laughing.

"See, it's not as easy as it looks, is it?" Padar says. "Now take these eggs and play elsewhere."

Alif and Amir hurry to the basement, trying not to drop the eggs. I follow. Overly religious guests give me the stink eye for standing next to a boy. Mâdar, especially, looks sneeringly at me. I'm sure I won't hear the end of it later, but for now, Amir is the closest thing to a girl — with a set of man boobies and a girlish voice.

Tap. Tap. Crack. Tap. Alif is focused and determined — if only he demonstrated such perseverance toward his school work, he wouldn't be taking most of his grade eleven courses with the dumb kids at school. He cracks my egg. He flings his arms in the air and lets out an ear-splitting laugh. The stench of victory is overwhelming.

"My turn," Amir says.

"I already kicked your ass!" Alif says.

Poor Amir. He always smells of failure. I'm reminded of that flap of foreskin at the tip of a penis — that little skin that Muslims are so eager to have surgically removed.

Alif places the remaining eggs back in the bowl and starts heading to the stairs. "I'm going to take this over to Ryan and Terry's."

"Can I come?" Amir asks.

"No!"

"Wait for me." I rise to follow Alif.

"No. You're not coming," he says.

Right as I'm about to free myself from Amir, he whines. "You and Alif . . . you're always picking on me. Why?"

I laugh. "Really? You want me to answer that?"

He looks up at me before dropping his head down.

I rise and smack the back of his head. "You're an easy target. Now man up!"

No laugh, no smile, no nothing.

I yank his arm. "Get up!"

Suddenly, he grabs me by both arms and thrusts me on the ground.

"What are you doing? Get the fuck off of me," I yell. He presses down on my mouth and gives me a look that's been building up for years.

I kick and sink my teeth in his hands, yet he doesn't stop. He climbs over me. His gaze holds mine before he pulls me up with a fistful of hair in his palm. He strikes me across the face, leaving a burning sensation on my cheek and ear.

Again, I try fighting. He uses one hand to grip my throat and the other to stop my arm from flinging. With mouth cracked open, body numb and tears raining down my face, I watch him peg me down onto one side as I give him the same look the sheep gave me as I watched Kâkâ Farhad slit its throat — a look of submission, disaster and failure.

Amir's nails rake down my flesh, stopping at my pants. He forces his fingers inside of me. Each time, his fingers go deeper, his voice becomes harsher and the look of animosity in his eyes grows bigger.

My vagina is sore. A burning sensation runs down my legs.

The rest of the night draws blank.

When the lights go out, I sneak into the bathroom. I strip down and look at myself in the mirror. My eyes follow the trail of dried blood that spreads down my thighs. My vagina is sore and inflamed. Amir's clawing and tearing of my flesh replays in my mind.

I step inside the shower and turn the dial to hot. I want to skin myself.

I begin to scrub until my flesh is raw, my veins are fully exposed and I am rid of his disease.

I scrub until I too resemble an animal that's hanging on hooks, with its head cleft from its body, its vessels severed and its guts splattered.

I step out; the entire bathroom is foggy. I wipe the misty bathroom mirror with my hands and stare at the horrific image that stares back at me — a monster that's thirsty for Amir's blood. I wrap a towel around my body and like a dishrag, I wring myself to dry.

Monster, Monster.

I am a monster.

CHAPTER

TWO

Saturday, March 18, 2000

I join my family for breakfast. It hurts to walk. As bad as the pain is, I bring my legs close together. I stand tall and take soft, slow steps.

I bite the inside of my lip to prevent myself from screaming as I lower down to sit next to Shabnam, the only seat available. I press my thighs to stop Shabnam from picking up on the smell of blood that's coming out of me.

Everything makes my vagina burn — peeing, walking, sitting and, especially, scrubbing. I avoid eye contact as I twist and turn to readjust my underwear that's riding up my crotch.

Mâdar is finishing up her telephone conversation.

"That was Farhad," she tells Padar once she sits. "He's asked to have Alif's goodbye party here."

"Goodbye party?" Padar asks before turning to Alif. "Did you know about this?"

Alif shakes his head.

Padar then looks at the rest of us. They all shake their heads, except for me. My fingers tremble; I cross my hands and place them on my lap. I'm not ready to face Amir; it was only yesterday that he sexually assaulted me. I bite my lip again, this time harder.

With the opening of our family restaurant, Padar forced Alif to quit his position at Bismillâh Halal Market. And now, Kâkâ Farhad is getting even by slightly changing the plans. It seems like getting even runs in his blood.

"I should've known he wouldn't take the news of losing Alif so lightly," Padar says. "Sanâj couldn't tell me this yesterday?"

"He said the shop is being fumigated. They're even going to have to spend the night here," Mâdar says.

My body flinches, just enough for Shabnam to notice. She scoots over. I dig my fingernails in my legs knowing that Amir is sleeping over. Even the pain in my vagina reignites.

"What's wrong with fumigating it the following week, *after* his party is done and over with?" Padar asks.

"They were reported to the health inspectors," says Mâdar.

Padar tries hard to conceal his smile. "It's about time. I've been telling him for months that if he doesn't get rid of the rodent problem, the next white man that walks in will. I also told him not to buy a shophouse, but once again, he didn't listen."

Any other time I'd be just as happy as Padar. The cluttered market carries a little bit of everything, slapped with an identity crisis, as it serves as a butcher shop, a bakery, a music store, a grocery store and a convenience store. Nothing is to be thrown out in this store; everything is hoarded and targeted for sale, even expired food items.

Seeing the look of annoyance on Alif's face, Mâdar tries to brighten his mood. "Well that's nice of your kâkâ, isn't it? Don't worry, I'll make sure it's extra special. Do you want to invite Ryan and Terry?"

"Darwâza ye kârwân wâ shod?" Padar asks.

"You're just as cheap and childish as your brother," Mâdar tells him. "They also plan to join us to garage sales tomorrow. You going to complain about that too?"

"No, because they'll be driving their own car."

Mâdar is obsessed with bargaining. If weekends aren't booked attending funerals, we spend family time hitting up yard sales.

Mâdar rushes to prepare qâboli palaw and mâhicha. Padar panics. "He's not providing the food?"

"Quiet, Kareem ăqâ. I already have a headache. He said he's bringing hamburgers, but we know what that means," Mâdar replies.

Kâkâ Farhad's poor customer service skills are also present in his hosting skills. Never have guests exited his home with a full stomach.

Mâdar pushes my and Shabnam's plates over to make room for a large strainer filled with carrots. She places it in front of us, along with a cutting board and two knives. "Peel the carrots and then slice them, but not too thin. When you're finished, start frying them. I'll add the raisins so you don't overcook them and turn it into wine," she says.

"Can I finish my breakfast first?" Shabnam asks.

"No," Mâdar says.

On the first chop, I slice a chunk of flesh off my finger.

Shabnam lets out a loud sigh. "How convenient," she says.

I bring my finger to my face and watch the blood flow.

Mâdar whacks the back of my head. "What are you staring at? Get out of here before you turn everything najis," she says. She starts to wash all the carrots, even the ones without blood on them.

"Maybe I should slice a finger off? Then I could finish my simiân and have time to study today," Shabnam says.

I walk up the stairs to our bedroom, not taking my eyes off my finger once. I close the door behind me and sit on my bed.

I watch the blood run down my finger. I squeeze it — enough that it looks like a red ribbon wrapping around my palm. I close my eyes and lick the blood, imagining that it's Amir's. Each lick tastes sweeter. I suck until the bleeding stops. I suck until the blood sets in and fills my body with rage.

At dinner, I sit across from Amir. I look at him, waiting for him to return the stare. He finally looks back, worriedly, knowing that I'm ready to face him.

"I'm going to miss you, son," Kâkâ Farhad suddenly tells Alif.

I look to see if there are any signs of jealousy in Amir's face. Instead, he's too busy grazing his food like a cow.

"Are you even chewing?" Kâkâ Farhad asks him. I laugh, louder than usual.

Khâla Wajma first glares at me and then at her husband. "Let our future sheik eat," she tells him.

Being reminded of his career path triggers me. It serves as his

48

shield, his guise to committing atrocious acts and walking away from them guilt-free.

"Looks like he ate a sheik," I blurt out.

All eyes turn to me as they wait to hear an apology. Even Alif is taken aback. I laugh and squirt a huge glob of ketchup onto my bun. I take a big bite, ketchup dripping onto my chin.

Once everyone has moved on I reach for a knife. I sweep it past Amir's face. He watches me as I reopen the cut on my finger.

Blood oozes out. I smile at the look of horror on Amir's face.

Mâdar eventually notices. "Wrap that finger or I'll cauterize it," she says.

After dinner, we watch a movie. Not surprisingly, Amir is the first to help himself to the popcorn.

My animosity for him makes it difficult to enjoy the film. I take my mini notebook out of my back pocket to distract myself. I doodle but still cannot help myself from writing about Amir.

Kids in class
pick on Amir's fatty ass.
"Lard-ass" and "porky ass,"
they say to harass.
"Son, let it pass,"
his mâdar tells his sorry ass.
She's also a dumb-ass
for not knowing he's a snake in the grass.

I slip my notebook back into my pocket. I look around in the hopes of finding another way to release my frustration. Nothing.

There's nothing that'll ease me. I watch my family — they're all deeply submerged into the film, except for Shabnam, who, with her textbook on her lap, is chewing the end of her pen. If I told them what Amir did to me, would they even hear it?

I then look over at my kâkâ, wondering the same about him, when suddenly, an idea occurs to me. As Amir tongue-fucks the salt on his fingers, I sneak into the kitchen to grab a cup before tiptoeing to the bathroom.

I pee into the cup. This time, the stinging does not bother me. I let the blood Amir left on me drip into the cup.

I make my way back into the kitchen to make a second batch of popcorn. I pour an extra ladle of butter to mask the colour of blood in my urine. Finally, I spit into the bowl and mix well.

I place the bowl in front of Amir without him even realizing it.

I smile as I watch him wipe the bowl clean.

"I don't feel so good. I think I need to lie down," Amir tells his mâdar partway through the film.

Khâla Wajma tucks in her grown-ass child in Alif's bedroom.

Once everyone's in bed, I feel at ease that Amir hasn't left the bedroom once. Yet, I still have trouble sleeping knowing that he's down the hall in Alif's room. I toss and turn. I look at the clock and it's 2:00 a.m. My bladder becomes full with urine for the third time.

After I'm finished, I turn the bathroom lights off when suddenly I see a shadow lurking in the dark.

It's Amir. His breath smells of piss. My body tightens and my chest pounds.

I turn the lights back on, he turns them back off. He places his hand over my mouth and pushes me into the bathroom. I fumble.

I punch him across the face. "Touch me and I'll fucking tell everyone."

He punches me back and pins me to the wall. His hands tightly wrap around my throat. "Who's going to believe you? Me or the fâyesha that showed her koss to Mr. Harvey?"

I gag as he plunges his penis down my throat.

I should be biting down on his dick. I should be ripping his balls right out of their sac. There's a lot I should be doing that I'm not because I hear "fâyesha" over and over. It's deafening, like every other derogatory title reserved for women. There's a shiver in my body and a clench in my jaw. No one has ever called me that.

He thrusts in me a few more times before disappearing back into the dark, leaving my throat parched and sore.

I form two fists and beat my head. I sob silently and curl into a ball in the corner of the cold bathroom. I wrap my arms around me, hiding my body in shame.

"Beh, is that you?"

Khâla Wajma is the last person I want to see right now.

"I thought I heard something. What's wrong?" she asks.

I ignore her. She takes my silence as invitation.

She puts her hand on my shoulder and asks, "Do you think it's from the popcorn? Come with me. I know just the thing that'll help you feel better."

We walk down the stairs and then past Kâkâ Farhad, who's

snoring loudly in the living room. Khâla Wajma grabs a cup from the kitchen cupboard and takes me down to the basement.

"Come lie down," she says.

I cry and shake my head as I refuse to lie on the floor that her son assaulted me on.

Khâla Wajma holds me in her embrace. I don't put up a fuss; I let her comfort me. She runs her fingers through my hair before placing a kiss on my forehead. I try to speak but my words are incoherent under the sobs.

"Let's get you calm first," she says. She lowers my head down, using one hand as a pillow and the other to straighten my legs.

She removes her hand from under my head and holds my hands before bringing them down to my sides.

"This is going to feel cold," she says as she lifts my shirt up and places the glass on my belly button, creating a suction.

Khâla Wajma removes the cup and places her fingers on my tense stomach. She presses down, rotating her fingers in a circular motion before placing the cup back onto my stomach. She repeats until my body loosens up. Her warmth calms me. I close my eyes but quickly open them as "fâyesha" repeats in my head.

I sit up, panting. Sweat drips off of me as my breathing intensifies.

"You're okay," she says, resting her hand on my cheek.

I look into her eyes, yet she cannot see me.

She gently lowers my body. "You'll feel better soon, I promise. There was something in that popcorn . . ."

She hums quietly as she presses down, this time harder. "You ready to come forward?"

"What?" I ask.

"You think I don't know you did something to Amir's popcorn?"

My lips tremble. I stutter.

Khâla Wajma places her hand over my mouth. "Not another word. Who's going to believe you? Amir, the *Quran* hâfez, or the fâyesha that showed her koss to Mr. Harvey?"

A golden stream runs down my leg. Khâla Wajma waits for me to finish urinating on myself. She smiles and walks away.

Was Khâla Wajma standing there the entire time? Why didn't she stop her son? How could she? I cry. No one will ever believe me. Who'd believe that Khâla Wajma would do such a thing?

All fingers point at me. Khâla Wajma never misses a prayer. I pulled my pants down to a married man. Amir can recite the *Quran*. I use my tongue to curse and challenge authority. Amir is a boy. I am a girl.

I am a disease.

CHAPTER

THREE

Friday, March 31, 2000

Across from Kâkâ Farhad's market is the Afghan Nomad, the only Afghani restaurant in the predominantly white neighbourhood of Kitsilano. The location is certainly not coincidental — if the restaurant is ever successful, Padar wants to rub it in his brother's face.

It's not only opening day today, but our first time seeing the restaurant too. Padar had planned to surprise the family.

We enter and experience culture shock. Padar didn't just bring Afghanistan to this section of Vancouver, he's rammed it down its throat — including ours.

Baluchi rugs, traditional Bokhara print carpets and a map of Afghanistan cover the walls, except for the main wall, which displays a mural of merchants, traders and pilgrims travelling the silk route on a camel caravan. A smaller replica of the mural also appears on the sign outside. Lights are replaced with fânous, and in the centre, a tiered, rustic chandelier hangs high. Hookahs, drums, robâb and flutes are displayed in one section of the restaurant, and lâjvard carvings of Bote Bâmiân in another. There are no chairs or tables, but rather heavy, intricate-patterned Afghani rugs, pillows and foam mattresses.

Beauty surrounds us, yet nothing can compare to the painting on the ceiling. We stop to admire it.

"This here is a combination of my fondest memories of Afghanistan, Bande-e Amir and Kabul's Bâgh e Vahsh. It's also my gift to each one of you," Padar says.

"Why is a dam named after Amir?" I ask.

"It's not. It means 'Commander's dam.' The name *Amir* means 'one who commands or rules,'" he says.

I spit gag.

A field of red tulips and Afghan pine trees look splendid against a background of barren snow-dusted mountains encircled by azure lakes. Eagles soar in the sky, butterflies in metallic and shimmering shades of blue and green appear beautiful in the sunlight, and mighty cheetahs and leopards drink from the lakes.

Padar looks at Alif. He says, "You're the golden eagle, Afghanistan's national bird. Known for their hunting and flying skills, they're also territorial. One day, this will all be your territory — when I'm no longer here, it'll be for you to serve so that you can provide for the family. It's also your job to watch over your sisters."

Padar expects a lot from a boy who can't even come home with a decent report card. Already, Padar's ruined the painting for me.

"Beh," he then says, "you represent Afghanistan's national

animal, the snow leopard. You're rare, beautiful and a dangerous beast."

I nod, not knowing what else to do. If he knew that I was far from the dangerous beast that people make me out to be, he'd compare me to the snow that's waiting to melt under the sun.

"Shabnam, you are the tulip, Afghanistan's national flower. Tulips carry great meaning in the story of Karbala. When Hosein died on the battlefields, tulips sprang from his blood. Even Khomeini's tomb is decorated in glass tulips to represent the martyrs who fought and died with Hosein. Tulips also mark the beginning of Nowruz, which is a time of rebirth," Padar says. He pauses to hold her hands. "Your blood is precious, similar to a red tulip, a red pearl."

As corny as that sounded, something about it gets me thinking. I hate flowers — they're for pussies. Flowers are dainty and pointless — they survive for a season and then fall limp to the ground. But the idea of allowing yourself to feel affects me. Maybe for once, I need to walk away from my image of a dangerous beast and show that I feel more than just anger. Maybe then, I will get my family to believe me.

"Then who's the Afghan nomad?" Alif asks.

"Me and Farzana. Like many Afghans fleeing their country to seek refuge, we didn't have a place we could just call home. We had to wander, move from place to place to protect our family," Padar says.

Padar then turns to Shabnam for compliments. "So, what do you think?"

"Thanks, Padar. I've never looked at it that way," Shabnam says.

"What about the rest of you? What do you think of the place?"

Mâdar nods, giving her approval. Alif mumbles, "It's nice," under his breath. When they look at me, I walk over to the front desk and pick up a pile of folded Afghani clothes that has my name written on them. "Is this what a snow leopard is supposed to wear?"

Right before the doors open for business, we all stare at one another, despising our uniforms.

Me and Shabnam have matching dresses on. They're long with a combination of different colours, patterns and handmade embroideries. The only difference is the colour of our scarves and flat shoes. Mine are leopard print and Shabnam's are solid red.

I raise my arms and let them fall. The dress is heavy; I don't know how Padar expects us to get any work done in these. "I look like a disco ball," I tell Shabnam.

"Just pray no one in school comes in to see us dressed like this," she says.

Padar and Alif both wear blue payran tombans with qara qols. Alif praises the hat. "This looks like something from Mostafa's farm."

Mâdar's outfit is the only normal-looking one. Hers is all black and made from a lighter, breathable material. Whether it's from the dim lighting or being dressed in all black, Mâdar looks like she's suddenly aged ten years. Her chiselled jawline appears more sculpted than usual, her cheeks are sunken and her rib cage sticks out.

Songs of Farhad Darya and Ahmad Zahir are playing faintly in the background as Padar flicks the "Open" switch on.

I find myself staring at the tulips. *I feel too* – far more than Shabnam could ever withhold.

Padar pushes me out the way. "Move. You can't just stand in the middle of the restaurant, you're going to block customers from coming in," he says.

Hours pass and not one single customer enters. I begin to sweat under my uniform. I crack open a window.

Mâdar turns the music down. "It's giving me a headache," she tells Padar. "I'll turn it back up once someone walks in."

Padar avoids eye contact. He's been avoiding looking at any of us for quite some time.

Suddenly, he reads aloud from the menu that I wrote. "The Afghan nomads, like many of us, are wanderers and travellers. Along with traders, merchants and pilgrims, nomads travel a series of trade routes that connect the West and the East. In the Afghan Nomad, we strive to deliver an authentic and memorable Afghan experience. Afghan cuisine is acclaimed for its blend of aromatic spices and succulent herbs. Discover the taste of turmeric, coriander, cardamom and rosewater in our dishes. Open your senses to the fresh scent of baked naan cooked daily in our tandoor. Dive into our tasteful mixtures of sauces and stews."

"Yeah, so?" I ask.

"Shouldn't you have written 'Dive into our tasteful blends and mixtures of qorma, ăsh and shorwâ'? I can't believe I didn't notice this before I had the menus printed," he says.

Luckily, Mâdar jumps to my defence. "Because that's the reason that's stopping people from coming in? Maybe if opening day was on the first of Moharram . . . like *we* had planned . . . then there'd be customers."

Padar, still avoiding eye contact, says, "First of Moharram is on a weekday. Even someone with poor business skills like Farhad would be foolish to do such a thing."

"I feel bad for Padar," Shabnam whispers to me, "but I'm happy that no one has seen me looking like this."

"That's what you're worried about? I'm fucking starving. I wonder if Padar's going to let us eat here for free."

"I'm sure you wouldn't like it if Mr. Harvey walked in right now either," Shabnam says.

"Forget Mr. Harvey. I'll never love another man again."

"Sounds like you feel sorry for yourself more than anything," Shabnam says right before she walks away.

Not until I look outside the window do I actually feel sorry for Padar. The streets are busy — there are lineups outside of coffee shops, burger joints and pasta restaurants. Doors open and close, yet not one head pokes in ours.

Padar will never admit this, but Kitsilano isn't ready for an Afghani restaurant. It's already enough that Kâkâ Farhad's shop is disrupting the peace. Besides, foreigners like us have their own designated areas to run a business. They're called Chinatown, Japantown and Main Street.

Suddenly, the door opens and a young couple enters.

"Please take your shoes off." Padar smiles, pointing at the shoe rack. The woman looks grossed out. The man laughs, thinking Padar is joking.

The white brooders are hesitant to order from our menu. "What's good?" the woman asks Padar.

Before Padar opens his mouth, the man speaks. "We'll have two vegetable samosas."

"There are no samosas here, sir. We're an Afghani restaurant, but if you like Indian food, I would recommend our kabobs. They're cooked with similar spices," Padar says.

"We're vegetarian," the man says.

Again, Padar tries to speak but is stopped.

"Perhaps we'll take a takeout menu to go?" the man says.

The rest of the day is no different. Customers drop in, ask for a takeout menu and then rush out the door. Some ask for samples, some ask to take photographs of our uniforms and a few show interest in our culture that is so exotic and foreign to them. I, however, continue to look up and obsess over the tulips.

I feel too, I whisper to myself.

CHAPTER

FOUR

Wednesday, April 5, 2000

All day in school I've been thinking of breaking my silence. *I need to tell someone.* I can't tell Padar or Alif. For once I feel ashamed to speak of my body to a man. I can't tell Shabnam either because then Padar will find out. I need to tell someone who'll listen. Who'll understand and make no judgments.

Mâdar will listen. She won't understand. She'll judge and blame me. She'll eventually tell Padar too. Even worse, she'll probably force the hijab on me — her way of "redeeming" my modesty. But if I don't tell someone, then it'll kill me.

Once home, I take my backpack off and look for Mâdar.

She's upstairs, taking a shower. I let myself in. "Mâdar?"

"Beh? Is that you?" she asks.

I take a deep breath and continue, "Can we talk? There's something I need to tell you."

She sticks her head out from behind the shower curtain. "Can it wait?"

My eyes water. "No."

"Fine, I'm coming out," she says.

She turns the dial off and sticks her arm out from behind the shower curtain. "Then pass me the towel," she says.

She dries herself. Right as she's about to draw the curtain, I hear a loud thump.

"Mâdar?" I ask.

There's no response.

I draw the curtain to find Mâdar's body jerking. Her eyes flicker and there's a small gash on her head.

I scream at the sight of blood pouring out of her. I run and open the door, shouting, "Someone call the ambulance."

Padar, Shabnam and Alif come running upstairs. Alif stands outside the door, knowing that Mâdar is naked.

"What happened?" Padar yells in my face as Shabnam dials for help.

I cry, "I don't know. She fell and must've hit her head."

"Wrap a towel around her," Alif says as he steps inside, with his hands over his eyes.

Mâdar is wheeled out on a stretcher and placed in the back of an ambulance. "I'm going with her," Shabnam tells Padar.

Driving to the hospital, no one has anything to say to one another. Instead, we listen to the violent sound of rain hitting the windshield.

We run to the emergency. Padar is already drenched in sweat; he wipes the sweat on his forehead.

"We're here to see Farzana Afshar," Padar tells the nurse at the cubicle.

The woman pulls Mâdar's file from the computer. "She's in the trauma room. Please wait in the family waiting area until a nurse or a doctor comes to speak to you," she says.

We meet Shabnam in the waiting area. Her posture is slumped and her gaze is down. She wipes the corners of her eyes, to prevent any blood falling to the floor.

"What'd they say?" Padar asks her.

"Nothing. They asked me to wait here," she says.

We do as we're told, sit and wait, not knowing what to expect, except to expect the worst. Alif is deep in thought. Shabnam looks like she wants to flood the place with her tears, and Padar can't keep still. He paces back and forth.

Hours pass. My eyelids grow heavy, when suddenly, a doctor pulls Padar aside.

"My apologies for keeping you waiting for so long. We've performed a few tests on your wife. Her vision, hearing, muscle strength, coordination and reflexes all appear to be fine. Her blood work, vitals and urine sample are also fine," the doctor begins.

Padar sighs in relief.

The doctor then leans in closer and says, "We are, however, concerned about her recurrent seizures."

Alif looks at Padar. He grits his teeth. The colour on Padar's face changes.

"She was having seizures every fifteen to twenty minutes.

We've managed to stop them and control her pain," the doctor says. He opens Mâdar's chart and reaches for a pen from his chest pocket. "Your daughter mentioned that your wife slipped in the shower?"

I jump in. "I was there when it happened," I say with a lump in my throat. "She must've hit her head on the ledge of the tub or something. All I heard was a big thump and then she was bleeding and having seizures."

The doctor scribbles down notes. "Did you see the fall?"

"No, she was behind a shower curtain."

"Was there something that triggered the fall?"

I shake my head, shamefully. Had I not gone in, Mâdar wouldn't have fallen.

"How long did the seizure last?"

"I don't know," I say, no longer holding back my tears.

The doctor pushes for answers. "A few seconds? Minutes?"

"Seconds, maybe," I say.

Alif grows impatient. He asks, "When can we see her?"

"I can only allow one person to see her, and only briefly. We usually don't allow anyone inside the trauma room due to confidentiality reasons," he says before directing the conversation to Padar. "I'd like to ask a few questions first."

Padar nods.

"Any history of seizures Farzana may have had in the past?"

"Yes," Alif answers with darting eyes.

Shabnam and I are confused. I, especially, am skeptical. Why are we learning this now? And why is Alif so angry with Padar?

Padar stutters. "She had a seizure three or four days ago. It only lasted for a few seconds and she seemed fine afterwards."

"Tell me more about that," the doctor says.

Padar's eyes water. "We got into an argument. She turned around to get away from me and then she tripped."

The doctor stops writing to look at Padar. He is better at hiding his skepticism than I am. "Did she see a doctor afterwards?"

Padar looks to the ground. "No," he says.

What's wrong with us? Why do we keep so many secrets?

The doctor jots down a few more notes and then proceeds. "Is she overall healthy? Any other medical concerns?"

"Yes, and nothing that I know of. She was also complaining about having migraines but neither of us thought much of it," Padar says.

"Any history of diabetes? Neurological problems? Slurred speech?"

Padar continues to shake his head.

"How about her family history?" the doctor asks.

"She didn't have family when I met her. Her parents passed away in Afghanistan."

"Anything she might've mentioned to you about their medical history?"

"No," Padar whispers.

"Has anything traumatic happened or was she undergoing more stress than usual?"

Padar pauses. He looks at each one of us before saying, "We recently opened up a family business."

"And how long ago was she having the migraines?" the doctor asks.

"Not long. Maybe a week or so," Padar says.

The doctor finally puts his pen down. "We'll need to keep her here overnight. There's a few more scans that need to be performed. Come with me, I'll take you to her."

We follow Padar, hoping the doctor will not notice. "You all can come, but you must wait outside," he tells us.

We watch Padar from the window. He places a hand on the side of Mâdar's face, careful not to wake her. He weeps before moving his hand down onto her leg, not wanting to let go.

It wasn't just Padar that turned a blind eye to Mâdar's health — I too have been busy feeling sorry for myself that I didn't once stop to ask Mâdar why her head ached so much.

"How is she?" Alif asks once Padar comes back, with the same look of anger on his face.

"I'll tell you in the car," Padar says.

We follow him to the car, eagerly waiting for what he has to say.

"How was she?" I ask Padar this time.

Padar starts his car and hurriedly drives off. "She was sleeping. We'll go see her first thing in the morning."

CHAPTER

FIVE

Tuesday, April 11, 2000

We enter Mâdar's room. It smells of urine. She's wet the bed again and a young nurse rushes in to change her bedsheets just as she sees us enter.

"She'll need a new gown too," Padar tells the nurse just as she's about to leave.

It's only been a few days since Mâdar decided to refuse treatment for her tumour. "I'm dying. I want to spend my final days present. I'm tired of vomiting . . . tired of feeling drowsy all the time," she told us.

"You're giving up. Do it for the children at least," was Padar's response.

Very badly, I wanted Padar to say, "Do it for me. Fight to stay alive for me. I need you." But such words are never exchanged between these two.

An hour passes and Mâdar has trouble keeping her eyes open.

"It's getting late and your mâdar is tired. Let's get going," Padar tells us.

"Why can't we just stay?" Alif asks.

"Your mâdar needs to rest. And it's Moharram. You have to go to mosque," Padar says.

Shabnam pleads. "Let's leave in a bit," she says.

We all want to be with Mâdar during this time, is that too much to ask? *For once, can we put a pause on being Muslim?*

"We go every fucking night. Why can't we miss one —" I try to say before Padar interrupts me.

"You're going to mosque and praying for your mâdar. Is that understood?" he shouts, loud enough that he draws a nurse to the room.

"I'm sorry, but visiting hours are over," the bitch tells us.

"I hope you're happy," Alif tells Padar before storming off.

Padar parks his car outside of the mosque. He keeps his seat belt on.

Alif gives him a dirty stare. "You're not coming?"

"No, I have to give your mâdar a bath," he says.

Alif lets out a scream and slams the passenger door shut.

Shabnam and I enter the women's section without greeting anyone. The room is crammed with children. We take a seat in the corner, trying very hard to ignore the noha that's being recited.

I look at my surroundings and fume over every second I have to be here. The place smells of death. Long black sheets of fabric cover the walls. A wall clock and two picture frames — one reading, "This life is only a test" and the other reading, "No sin is greater than ghaybat" — are hung on the wall. In between the pictures is a shelf that consists of several books, titled *Stairway to Heaven, The Staircase to Heaven, The Path to Heaven, The Way to Heaven, Shia vs. Sunni* and many more.

The women — who are forbidden from pampering themselves during this holy month — look like men with their bushy eyebrows, thick moustaches and coarse facial hair. They stare at one another and whisper back and forth until the long-bearded, freakish-looking sheik enters the men's room. He climbs up three stairs to sit on the minbar. The women watch the sheik through a television screen.

The sheik clears his throat, loudly, into the microphone. All the men are quiet, readying themselves for the sermons, unlike in the women's room, where more time is needed. Khâla Wajma rises to sprinkle rosewater over our heads, which I like to think is to mask the odour of gossip. I imagine drowning her in a tub of rosewater.

"Water," the sheik says. After a long and dramatic pause, he continues, "Not a drop of water was to be given to Imam Hosein and his followers."

"I don't care," I say. Why would I care about a death that happened centuries ago? I'd rather be with Mâdar than attend mosque every night to witness the women wail and the men hit themselves with chains.

"Then care. Mâdar would want you to," Shabnam tells me.

I want to elbow her, but I don't. I've been hearing this a lot lately — "Do it for your mâdar" or "Mâdar would want that." I don't like being told what to do, but for Mâdar, I'll do anything.

I smile as I imagine Mâdar nagging in my ear, "You must listen, both with your ears and your heart."

"On the seventh of Moharram, when water was completely cut off, the children, raising their plastic glasses high in the air, looked to Hosein's daughter, Sakina, for water," the sheik says.

Chit-chat is immediately put on pause and taken over by whimpers. Women draw their veils closer to themselves, preventing others from seeing them cry. Some hide their faces in tissue paper. Some cry lightly, not wanting to blow their cover for wearing mascara. Others wail in pain, with a blob of mucus hanging down their nose as proof.

The lights dim. Children search for their mâdars as they become fearsome of the darkness and the eerie sound of crying.

"Sakina, with her empty mashk in hand, headed toward her uncle, Abbas," the sheik continues. When the name *Abbas* enters the mourners' hearts, the mucus hangs lower.

I think of Mâdar and her refusal to drink water at the hospital. Everywhere is water, yet not one drop touches her parched lips. Her breakfast, lunch and dinner are always served with a cup of water and always it's returned untouched.

Once I imagine Mâdar occupying the role of Abbas, the legend of Moharram moves me. *Mâdar would be so proud.*

"'Uncle Abbas, will you please bring the children some water?' Sakina asked. Abbas knew he wouldn't come back alive, but for her, he was willing to sacrifice his life," the sheik says.

The beating on their chests begin, not giving the slightest care that their children's cries are growing louder. The women cry uncontrollably, hoping that their eyes will bleed with pain.

"He bid farewell to his brother, Hosein, before pleading with their enemies. Seeing that they would not reason, with his alam in hand, Abbas headed straight for the Euphrates River. Dying from thirst, once at the river, he formed a cup with his hands and filled them with water. But, the thought of the waterless children crushed his heart. 'Not until the children drink!' he shouted as he spilled the water," the sheik says. By now, I am doing backstrokes in a pool of snot.

I imagine Mâdar, like Abbas on horseback, bidding farewell to a group of bloodthirsty men that are shooting arrows at her. Mâdar, with a shield tied to her back and a sword wrapped around her hips, appears as a kick-ass warrior.

The sheik stops to listen to the cries of men and women. He says, "Abbas filled Sakina's mashk with water, just like she had asked. Just then, soldiers chopped his arms off. Armless, he placed the water bag in his mouth, pressing tightly with his lips. But when an arrow pierced right through the bag, emptying out all of the water, he dropped to his knees. 'Do you have no mercy for the family of the Prophet?' were his final words before an arrow martyred him."

The sheik takes his hands to his eyes and cries until he can't cry anymore.

Mâdar is greater than Abbas!

Cheated by the story of Abbas, I tune out. I will not allow Mâdar's story to end tragically. Instead, I close my eyes and take control of my dream. I visualize Mâdar as dexterous. Her hauberk, sword and shield shine. Her Herculean arms and legs are tanned and dripping in sweat. Every inch of her body is sculpted

73

and ready for combat — even her horse is mighty as it gallops and the ground beneath it cracks.

Wicked soldiers come at Mâdar from all sides. They shoot arrows and spears at her. Blades whoosh above her head, yet nothing can get in Mâdar's way. She strikes and blocks the opponents' every move. Cling! Clang! The slamming of swords is heard from a distance.

Blood flows like water, enough to cover the entire desert. Rage oozes out of Mâdar's pores. Some of her enemies flee, some cry out for their mâdars as they bleed out and some drop their swords before her, falling onto one knee and begging for her forgiveness.

The commander especially wants to conquer Mâdar — he rides on a war elephant encrusted in gold armour while his men parade around him with swords, axes and lances in hands.

Mâdar lets him come closer before she takes her helmet off. Her long black hair falls down her back. It whirls, even though there is no wind. The sudden realization that the warrior is a woman causes the commander to put a tear in Mâdar's clothes. She rebuts by cutting off both of the elephant's front feet with one sway.

The commander comes tumbling down, with his sword still clenched in his grip. Mâdar, screaming with all her might, knocks the blade free of his hand and jumps off her horse, making a dent in the earth. She beheads him, quickly and effortlessly. A fountain of blood soaks her face. She raises her sword high in the air and shouts.

I open my eyes, smiling. But my smile fades into a frown at the realization that I'm still at mosque. I try to escape back into my imagination, but this time, the sheik is yelling, forcing me to follow the story of Abbas again.

"Hosein buried his brother and returned to his camp, holding his brother's blood-drenched alam. From that day on, Sakina never complained of thirst," the sheik says.

I close my eyes, refusing to open them until I dream of Mâdar again. This time, I see things I don't wish to see. This time, Mâdar's legs are quivering and her breathing is heavy. Realizing the weightiness of the sword, she lets it drop before her body slams hard against the dirt. I let out a harsh yell and run toward her. The closer I get to her, the smaller her body appears. I flip her over, wipe the dirt off her face and take a good look at her before burying my head in her chest. Her warrior clothes have been replaced with a hospital gown, her muscles have dissolved and most of her hair is gone.

Suddenly, a dozen other soldiers appear.

"They're coming," I whisper in her ear.

Mâdar lays there, in the bloody and intestine-filled battlefield, limp and lifeless.

"Wake up," I say as I shake her body. I lift her head and kiss her lips.

Mâdar stands and falls until she's able to stand tall and proud. She tightens her head scarf and climbs onto her horse. As she rides, the sun appears and shines directly on her.

Mâdar kills the remaining soldiers before she looks at me. She smiles and then rides off.

The sheik screams, bringing me back to present-day reality. "Abbas, our alam keeper, was martyred!"

The alam, a long pole dressed in green fabric with a big hand placed on the very top, is passed along in the men's room. Loud chants are screamed by the men, with Alif's voice being the loudest. Then the alam is sent to the women's room.

"To whom does this unattended alam belong to?" men and women shout, to which is replied the following: "This unattended alam belongs to us! Oh Abbas, oh Abbas! We love you, Abbas."

I stare at the great hand. Mâdar too has great hands, even though they are now wrinkly and feeble. With her hands, she takes great care of us. She scrubs the dirt off of our backs, she fattens us up, she keeps us warm and in times of frustration, she disciplines us.

A sudden rush takes over me. I'm tired of being a disease. *I feel too,* I think. I make my way toward the alam. It's a stampede; young children can easily be crushed if they aren't kept back. Movement is difficult and minimal as women throw themselves onto the alam, tightly latching onto it and preventing other women from visiting the alam.

My hands meet the alam and I can no longer maintain my composure. I let myself feel. I clench my teeth. With flaring nostrils, tightening throat and burning eyes, I pray for Mâdar. Gut-wrenching tears rip through my chest.

PART 2 – شبنم

SHABNAM

CHAPTER

SIX

Saturday, March 4, 2000

A month of nagging has finally convinced Padar to share stories of my birth mâdar with me. I know nothing about this woman, except that she passed away from blood loss due to a retained placenta. In fact, I know more about the rumours of her death than anything. In one version, I ripped her in half, leaving her to bleed out. In another version, I ate her insides before entering the world. And in another, I ripped through her stomach with my sharp teeth. Yet in every rumour the explanation for my tears of blood remains the same: I weep birth mâdar's blood as punishment for taking her life.

Early in the morning, we disappear to the mall.

Padar greets Jaspreet, who smells of coriander and cumin seeds. He hands Padar a white slip of paper. Padar pulls a pencil out of his pocket once we sit down. He brings his head close to mine and says, "Mojda loved birds, her favourite was the lovebird — she probably owned at least five of them, all which she named.

I wasn't too crazy about them; they never stopped chirping, especially first thing in the morning."

He fills in a number and continues, "Those birds sure did love her back. Her one bird, Firishta, never wanted to get off of her shoulder.

"Your turn, you pick a number," Padar then says.

Before I even get a chance, Padar fills in number fifty-two.

"Your birth mâdar was so beautiful," he suddenly says. "The image of her in my mind is so vivid. I can still remember how she made me feel."

I force a smile. *Then why are curses passed down to me?*

According to Padar, my birth mâdar didn't cry blood. She didn't have green eyes either. Yet, as desirable as green eyes are in my culture, they're no longer beautiful when they're tainted by red tears. "Jinn," I've been called by my Afghan community. Created from a smokeless flame, these demonic beings are harmful to humans. "Take her to the shrine of Imam Hosein" or "Take her to Châh e Zamzam," I heard women at mosque whisper in Mâdar's ear during most of my childhood.

I feel even more cursed next to Beh and Alif. Even though she's only thirteen, with her slim figure, red plump lips, oval-shaped eyes and jet-black hair complimenting her fair skin, Beh looks like a runway model. Even Alif appears more feminine. With my broad shoulders and short waist, people mistake me for a boy from the back.

"For someone so beautiful, you'd think she wouldn't birth a monster," I say.

"Look at me. You're not a monster. Don't ever call yourself that, you understand? Mojda fell in love with you the second she held you. To her, your red tears of pearl were as beautiful as the morning dew, which is why she named you Shabnam."

If Padar's eyes weren't glued to his lottery ticket, he'd see that I have a look of disappointment on my face.

"Why haven't you told me that before?" I ask.

"I thought you knew what your name meant," he says.

"No, not that. Why haven't you told me that my birth mâdar named me?"

Padar mumbles, "I don't know," under his breath as he fills in more numbers.

I stop him from rushing over to Jaspreet by taking the slip away from him. "Can you stop? This is very important to me."

He sighs. "I'll stop. I'm sorry." He brings his chair in closer and faces me. "It wasn't meant to be a secret. I didn't know it meant this much to you."

"I guess what I'm trying to say is that I wish I had known that someone other than *you* found my tears beautiful."

"You're wrong about that. Farzana would've named you Shabnam too, you know she would," he says.

I cross my arms and look away. "It's always just been a mess to clean for her."

"Yes and no. Blood stains, and that's neither your fault nor hers. But, here's a story you need to hear," he says as he takes the slip back. "After you were born, I had to run away with you.

I took you away from Mojda's family because I knew if I stayed, there'd be talk of shafâ. Then I met Farzana, and it wasn't until she came along that I started to believe that another woman could be a mâdar to you. In these sixteen years of being married to her, not once has she seen your tears as a disease, as something that needs curing."

"Then what about all the medical exams?" I ask.

"Those were all my terrible ideas, not hers. Even your blood bath was my idea. The older you got, the more you bled. I was worried; I didn't want you losing too much blood," he says.

"Terrible?" I ask.

"I brought you to Canada to get you away from the sorcery. What I didn't know was that the doctors here saw you as a medical freak show," he says.

I finally join Padar to see Jaspreet. He collects his winnings — a crisp five-dollar bill that he folds to fit in his wallet.

"I feel like we're betraying Mâdar by gambling," I say.

"We've already betrayed her," he says. "Let's go for ice cream. We'll have to finish it in the car though. Farzana has garage sales lined up for today."

I feel bad for doing this, I really do. Mâdar has never called me or made me feel like an andar. But it's also selfish of her that I'm not allowed to know anything about birth mâdar. *Why is she so threatened by a dead woman?*

"So that's it? Mâdar loved birds?" I ask, not impressed by Padar's willingness to cut this short.

"Birth mâdar," Padar corrects me. "Blood or not, your mâdar

is Farzana, and she's a smart woman. She'll know we're up to something if we don't leave soon."

On the drive home, I look at Padar, hoping he'll pass the time by sharing more stories. Instead, he wipes ice cream from his chin with his sleeve and fiddles with the cassette player.

We pull into the driveway. Mâdar, Alif and Beh are already outside, waiting for us.

Before their seat belts are fastened, Padar plays his favourite cassette, *Greatest Hits of Ahmad Zahir.*

"Turn that off before I kill myself," Beh says.

"You're so dramatic," Alif tells her.

"Ahmad Zahir was an icon. He was referred to as 'King' in Afghanistan," Padar says.

Kicking the back of the driver's seat, Beh says, "I already know and I don't care. Turn that off!"

Beh is the spitting image of Mâdar. If Beh is disrespectful to Padar, it's because she's learned it from Mâdar.

"He was assassinated —" Padar continues.

I hate to agree with Beh, but whatever the reason, Zahir's heroism didn't make his music sound any better. "Can we listen to something else, please?" I ask Padar.

"How about the bazaar song?" Beh is quick to add.

"Now that's an idea," laughs Padar.

"What about your poem that you've been working on for

weeks? Don't you want to rehearse for us before you present it to the entire school?" I ask Beh.

"I don't need to rehearse. I'm going to win," she says.

She's probably right — Beh is most likely to take home the award for best poet at our school's annual poetry competition. I don't know who she inherited it from, but Beh is a talented writer.

Padar clears his throat and sings, "Padar's walnut in shell. Padar's stay-at-home daughter. Padar will go to bazaars, big and small, only to buy you earrings of your preference."

I roll my eyes and give in. "I am no walnut in shell. I am no at-home-stay daughter. Don't go to any bazaars, Padar. Don't buy me earrings of my preference, Padar," I sing.

I can see Padar smiling from the rear-view mirror. Mâdar is also enjoying herself; she's laughing and appears relaxed.

"Padar's walnut in shell. Padar's stay-at-home daughter. Padar will go to bazaars, big and small, only to buy you a necklace of your preference," Padar sings, moving his head to the beat.

Alif laughs. We are now all pressing hard against our bellies.

"I am no walnut in shell. I am no at-home-stay daughter. Don't go to any bazaars, Padar. Don't buy me a necklace of my preference, Padar," I sing.

"Padar's walnut in shell. Padar's stay-at-home daughter. Padar will go to bazaars, big and small, only to buy you a ring of your preference," sings Padar as he takes one hand off the steering wheel and dances.

"I am no walnut in shell. I am no at-home-stay daughter. Don't go to any bazaars, Padar. Don't buy me a ring of my preference, Padar."

"Padar's walnut in shell. Padar's stay-at-home daughter. Padar will go to bazaars, big and small, only to buy you a husband of your preference," sings Padar. Now both of his hands are off the wheel.

I jump out of my seat to steer the wheel and sing, "I am no walnut in shell. I am no at-home-stay daughter. But go to bazaars and buy me a husband of my preference, Padar."

I sit back in my seat and smile. For some strange reason, Padar only likes to sing the "bazaar song" to me — maybe because he doesn't think that anyone in their right mind would marry Beh. The ancient song, according to Padar, was sung by padars to their single daughters, with the assumption that all women dream of being swept off their feet. Throughout the song, the daughter is supposed to play coy up until she hears the word *husband*. Foolish Afghan parents, they think marriage solves all of women's woes.

After driving around, passing one garage sale then the next, Padar finally spots one that's worth parallel parking his car for. Colourful balloons are tied here and there to further attract people's attention.

"They look rich," Mâdar says as she scopes the house. "All their stuff must be new and clean. We won't have to worry about any bedbugs."

Hardly ever do we buy from garage sales. Instead, we treat them more like an art gallery.

As Mâdar makes her way to the kitchen supplies and upholstered furniture, Alif runs to the bicycles, and Beh, to the collection of records and books.

Mâdar rummages through the pots and pans.

"What are you going to do with that? Your cupboards are filled with them," Padar tells her as she examines another cast iron pot set.

Alif tries on a helmet before spotting a table filled with tennis rackets, key chains and golf balls. He drops the helmet and rushes over to the table. Beh takes his lead and Padar follows.

"This isn't even worth a penny," Padar tells Alif as he holds a wooden slingshot up to Beh's face.

Before Padar leaves to look around, he tells Beh, "Don't touch anything."

Beh cannot help herself. She touches everything.

"Oh, cool," Alif says, as he holds up a keychain that says: WHEN I DIE, BURY ME UPSIDE DOWN, SO THE WORLD CAN KISS MY ASS.

Beh snatches it from his hand. "Give it," she says.

"Padar will never buy you that," Alif says.

"I know."

"You want it that bad?" he asks.

Beh nods.

Alif pays for the key chain and places it in Beh's palm. She quickly tucks it in her pocket. I smile. Regardless of the hair pulling, biting and blows to one another's heads, Beh and Alif share a beautiful relationship. Beh is the little brother Alif always longed for, and Alif is the boy living inside of Beh. Even though neither of them have treated me like their half-sibling, I still know that some bonds are closer than others. They're inseparable, just as their inauthentic Muslim names suggest:

Alif, the first letter of the Arabic alphabet — ا

Beh, the second letter of the Arabic alphabet — ب

And then there's the misplaced:

Shabnam, the girl that cries blood – شبنم

I continue to walk, in the hopes of finding something that interests me. I roam about until my eye catches something from afar. It's Padar, who in a corner, hidden by armoires and rocking chairs, is looking into a vintage birdcage.

I take a seat next to him. He's humming to a lovebird that's asleep on a swing.

He taps his finger on the edge of the cage, trying to wake the animal. Once its eyes open, the bird tilts its head to one side and chirps. Padar's smile welcomes the bird to fly over and lick his finger. "This bird reminds me exactly of Firishta. Strange that we see this today," he tells me.

"Let's buy it," I say.

He looks up at me and smiles. His eyes water as I know he's thinking of birth mâdar, his first love, his only memory of happiness in a marriage.

CHAPTER

SEVEN

Saturday, March 4, 2000

"That bloody animal won't stop chirping," Mâdar says over dinner. "I'm still trying to figure out why Kareem ăqâ suddenly decided to buy a bird."

I've always found it fascinating when Mâdar speaks of Padar in the third person, especially when he's in the same room.

Mâdar gets up from the dining table to throw a cover over the bird's cage. Only a few hours have passed since we brought Firishta home and already she's fed up. I look at Padar, hoping for a reaction.

"It has a name," I finally say.

"What?" Mâdar asks, with a raised brow.

"Our bird has a name, and it's not 'bloody animal.'"

"Shabnam, stop," Padar says.

"We named her Firishta, after birth mâdar's favourite love-bird," I say. Alif and Beh look up at me in bewilderment as Padar shouts, "Shabnam!"

Mâdar wipes her mouth with a napkin and throws it over her plate. "So that's why you bought a bird?" she asks Padar.

"Shabnam wanted to know more about her birth mâdar, that's all," Padar says.

"You're not answering the question," Mâdar says.

"You're reading too much into this. It was only a harmless story."

"It's one thing to share a 'harmless' story and another to bring a bird into this house because you can't get over your —" Mâdar starts to say before I interrupt.

"Buying the bird was my idea," I say.

Mâdar looks disappointed, more so with me than Padar. "Why?" she asks.

"I'm seventeen years old, Mâdar, and I know nothing about my birth mâdar. I wasn't trying to . . . We weren't trying to hurt you. Padar had just shared a story about Mâdar's love for lovebirds, and coincidentally, the same day, we came across a lovebird. I thought it was a sign."

Mâdar laughs. "The same day? Why wasn't I told about any of this?" she asks Padar before looking at me. "A sign of what exactly? *Blood isn't everything,* Shabnam. I'm your mâdar."

"Farzana, please," Padar says. "It only happened today and I was meaning to tell you."

"Don't 'please' me, Kareem. You should've thought about how that would make me feel. It's not like the ghost of your dead wife isn't already haunting me," Mâdar says.

"I'm sorry. First thing tomorrow morning, I'll get rid of it. I'll take it to —" Padar tries to say, but I interrupt him.

"What? No, you can't."

Everyone falls silent. Mâdar and Padar look down at their plates. Alif looks out the window and Beh gives me a death stare.

"Your padar isn't the only one with harmless stories," Mâdar suddenly says after what appears to be the longest moment of silence. "Did I ever tell you how he acquired the nickname Mullah Nasreddin Hodja?"

Padar slams his fist on the table. "This is going too far," he says.

Mâdar occasionally refers to the tales of Mullah Nasreddin Hodja, but never once has she compared him to Padar. A philosopher from Iran, he was known for his halfwitted anecdotes. I, personally, enjoy listening to them; he reminds me of a Middle Eastern version of Mr. Bean. But now that his stories are being used as a weapon against Padar, I'm not too sure how I'll feel about him anymore.

"This one time, Mullah Nasreddin Hodja wanted to sell his donkey," Mâdar begins boisterously. "This old donkey was lazy, stubborn and ate way too much, so he vowed to sell it at an auction for a finer one that required less spending. Before he set off, he promised his wife that he'd buy her the finest gold with the money saved. His poor wife was against the idea, but once Nasreddin had his mind set, nothing could get in the way."

Padar gives Mâdar a disapproving look, yet she doesn't stop.

"The entire way, Nasreddin kicked and beat his donkey to move faster, but the animal was stubborn, refusing to move until it was fed and hydrated. On their tenth break, Nasreddin realized that his bag sat lightly on his shoulders. Food and water were scarce. 'You selfish donkey, what am I to do on the way back?' he shouted. Tired and hungry, Nasreddin placed his head on a big rock and cried himself to sleep.

"The next morning, they rose early to conquer the heat of the desert. Finally, after five gruelling hours, they arrived at their journey's end. While his donkey looked well-fed and well-rested, Nasreddin's throat was so dry that it hurt to speak. Half asleep, Nasreddin dug deep to find the energy to brag about his donkey to the auctioneer. 'There is no other donkey greater than this one. He's strong, stronger than an army of men. His legs and back can carry and withstand the capacity of twenty men. He can travel for days, without stopping once. He can run faster than the wind,' he said, as if reading from a script," Mâdar says.

I look over at Padar. His eyes are glued to his plate again.

"The day faded into evening and not once did Nasreddin make a bid. Soon, the villagers began to vanish, leaving only Nasreddin and a handful of villagers behind. The auctioneer began to worry; every now and again he'd look over at Nasreddin to see if he was still awake. Finally, only two donkeys remained — one of which was his own," Mâdar continues.

Mâdar pushes her plate, crosses her legs and places her elbows onto the table. "Finally, his donkey was brought to the stage." Mimicking an auctioneer's voice, Mâdar says, "'And now, saving the best for the last. This donkey that stands before you wise men has a wise look in its eyes. It's obedient and holds its head up high.'

"Nasreddin then noticed a look in the donkey's eyes that was never apparent before. Then he looked at the donkey's head and realized that its head was held up high. Catching the crowd by surprise, Nasreddin jumped off his seat and made the first bid."

"He's smart," I say, only to lift Padar's spirits. "The other bidders didn't know it was Nasreddin's donkey. Maybe, he was doing all of this only to get the show started?" I look over at Padar. He gives me a look, enough to tell me that I'm not making things any better.

"Don't interrupt," Mâdar says. "Then the auctioneer says, 'Look at the donkey's build. His legs are powerful. He can carry a heavy load, climb steep hills and run in great speed.' Nasreddin then looked at his donkey and nodded his head in agreement. He bid higher, and by this point, the villagers were all off their seats, bidding and fighting over the donkey."

Mâdar laughs and continues, "'Two and a half lirâ,' called a villager. 'Three!' yelled Nasreddin. 'Four!' 'Five!' 'Six!' The bids got higher and higher. Even the auctioneer was surprised that Nasreddin continued bidding. Overcome with greed, the auctioneer pushed one last time. He said, 'I have never seen any donkey wear such a smooth coat. The colour on the coat matches nicely with its white boots.'"

Mâdar is now wiping away tears of laughter, unlike Padar, who's stopped listening. By now, all of our appetites have vanished.

"Nasreddin looked at his donkey and admired its coat. He bid and bid. Uproar struck. Finally, he bid ten lirâ and eleven qurush on his own donkey. Not only did he buy his own donkey, but he spent more than he had planned. The auctioneer was in complete shock. Never had he come across a fool like Nasreddin," Mâdar says.

"He realized that his donkey was worth more than what it was being sold for," Padar finally says.

"*His wife's* point exactly," Mâdar says. "*My* point, exactly. Don't bring something into this house when you already have so much to be thankful for."

Padar takes his plate and throws it. Shards of glass are scattered in every direction. Beh, Alif and I look at one another in complete shock. Neither of them care to pick up the broken pieces of our parents' marriage, leaving me to clean up.

No child thinks that their parents would be better off divorced, except for me. Mâdar and Padar have fought during most of their marriage so that they've forgotten what a normal conversation looks like. "We're not fighting. We're just talking," Padar would tell us when we were younger. But now that we're older, no cover-ups or explanations are required. Padar is indiscreet, claiming, "This is marriage. It's what married couples do."

This isn't what married couples do, and if this is what marriage is like, then I never wish to be married. As much as Mâdar and Padar ridicule white people for getting separated or divorced, exploring the joys of meaningless affairs and constantly finding themselves in custody battles, I sometimes wish I was born in a white family — at least white parents believe in marriage counselling.

"Shabnam, sit. Farzana can clean the mess later."

Padar reaches for another plate and towers it with food. He picks up his fork, takes a few bites and chews, bit by bit. "My turn," he says.

"Once upon a time there was a man named Jawad who belonged to a small village with poor people," he begins, again stopping to grab a few bites to eat. "The people around him were growing sicker and sicker by the day and Jawad was growing tired of seeing his people die."

Mâdar pretends not to listen; she looks away.

"Shabnam, pass me the water jug," Padar says. He fills up his cup and drinks the entire glass in one gulp.

"His neighbour," he continues, "a widowed woman with several young children, all who were too young to work, was left with no other choice but to provide for her family. The stress was overwhelming, impacting her physically and mentally. She began to have kidney failure. This neighbour wasn't just any neighbour — Jawad saw her grow up before his eyes. Her children were also the future of their village, so Jawad presented her with the greatest gift anyone could ask for: his kidney. 'I have two anyway,' was his answer.

"The following month there was a knock on his door, and to his surprise, it was his neighbour again. 'Please,' she begged, 'I need a lung. Without a lung, I won't be able to provide for my family . . . our village.' Jawad, still trying to recover from his surgery, took a deep breath and said, 'I'll donate one lung to you. I have two anyway.' Two weeks later, she knocked on his door again. This time, she was begging for an eye. Now trying to recover from his previous operations, he replied by saying, 'I'll donate one eye to you. I have two anyway.'

"Poor Jawad, it didn't end there for him — one knock led to another and then another until he was left with one arm, one leg and one ear. The widowed woman and her family were thriving because of Jawad's generosity. Even his village was prospering. But poor Jawad. He didn't live much longer to see any of it happen."

"So I'm the widowed woman? What have I not given you?" Mâdar shouts.

"What have I not given you?" Padar shouts back. "I can chop myself into a million pieces for you and it's still not enough. I don't know what more I can say or do to prove my love for you and this family."

"Stop with the secrets. You can start with that." Mâdar is surprisingly a lot calmer than Padar.

"It's only a secret because of your jealousy," Padar says, continuing to shout.

Mâdar is now furious. A conflict of emotions arises, making it difficult to tell whether Mâdar is laughing or crying. "What did you just say to me? You take that back, right now, Kareem."

"She's dead for crying out loud!" Padar says before he slams the back of his head onto his chair.

We all fall silent as we watch our parents cry. Something so little turns into something so big with these two. It's exhausting. It's heartbreaking. I don't know who's at fault when both of them stoop to one another's level.

Suddenly, Firishta begins to chirp loudly. It flaps its wings and flies around, knocking down its feed cup. Bird food mixed with feathers scatter all over Mâdar's clean floors.

Mâdar blows her nose and wipes her tears on a napkin. She says, "Alif, get rid of that damn bird. I never want to see that thing in my house ever again."

"You even think about getting up from your seat and you'll have to answer to me," Padar tells a passive Alif. He's probably used to being caught in the middle of their arguments by now.

Padar then turns to Mâdar and says, "The bird is staying. For Shabnam."

"Fine," Mâdar says as she gathers herself. "If you're going to bring the ghost of your past into this house, then so will I."

Just when I thought Padar couldn't scream any louder, he lets out an ear-splitting holler. "How dare you?"

Padar forms a fist. He raises his arm in the air as if he's going to strike Mâdar. Alif jumps out of his chair and pushes Padar. He falls down, onto the pieces of glass.

"What is she talking about, Padar?" I ask.

He does not answer. He gets up, looks at Alif with hurt in his eyes and slams the front door. He drives off and doesn't come home until midnight.

CHAPTER

EIGHT

Sunday, March 5, 2000

Mâdar and Beh are up at the crack of dawn for Alif's circumcision mehmouni. I wake up to the smell of Mâdar's baking; I squeeze my stomach to stop it from growling.

I hesitantly walk down the stairs, not knowing what to expect from Mâdar. Most of the work is complete, except the qaymâq chây. I don't know if I should be relieved or worried.

Mâdar transfers the chây from one pot to another, forming little air bubbles. I wipe the sweat off my cheeks from the cloud of steam.

"Salâm. Why didn't you wake me?" I ask Mâdar.

She glances past me and ignores me, a clear indication that she's still upset with me over Firishta. Beh is also ignoring me, which she usually does.

Fine, I'll ignore them too.

I walk straight to the fridge to fix myself breakfast. I spread butter onto my pita and sprinkle sugar over it, making sure to get it all over the kitchen counter. I choose not to clean up after myself. Mâdar looks scornfully at me as I walk past her and sit at the dining table.

Padar makes his way down the stairs. Curious to see the tension between Mâdar and Padar, I make my way back to the fridge to pour myself a glass of milk.

Padar greets Mâdar, she greets him back. They then speak to one another as if nothing ever happened.

Mâdar holds a pastry up to Padar's face. "Take a bite. Tell me if you think it needs more sugar," she says.

He savours every bite and says, "No, it's perfect."

I look at them in confusion. I stare at Padar; he's now avoiding me too.

I slam the fridge door and grab my breakfast, wanting to finish it in my bedroom.

"Where do you think you're going? You know better than to eat upstairs," Padar says. "Get over here and help your mâdar and sister."

Mâdar hands me a stack of napkins and directs me to the cupboard with her fancy silverware. "Fold," she says.

Folding napkins into a triangle shape and then wrapping it around the cutlery is a task I've always hated. "I don't see why we just can't place the napkins beside the spoons and forks?" I ask Mâdar.

Instead, Padar answers. "You can't expect the guests to help themselves. They need to be served and attended to."

I glare at Padar. Why is he defending her? The two were down each other's throats yesterday, yet they gang up on me?

"Then get Alif to do it. It's his party," I say.

"Stop whining," Beh says. "You're only jealous that we didn't throw you a party once you started bleeding out of your vag—"

"Stop being a disease," Padar tells her, finally coming to his senses.

Beh's right, and it hadn't occurred to me until now. Except I'm not jealous, I'm furious. I renounce my culture for favouring males over females. When a girl reaches puberty, she gets lessons on how to behave the "proper way," served with litee and châwa on the side.

If being born an Afghani girl is a curse, growing into an Afghani woman is a bigger curse. I disapprove of my changing and growing body, especially since women's bodily — *and bloody* — leakages are flat out considered najis. We're forbidden from praying, touching the *Quran*, touching the deceased and having sex.

I wonder if Ayatollah Sistani would label me as najis for crying blood?

I'll never forget Mâdar's introduction to tampons versus pads. "This is a tampon. If I ever see you using this, you'll have to answer to me. Never go near this until you're married," she said.

"Why?" I asked.

"If you use a tampon, you won't bleed on your wedding night. Your husband and your in-laws will think that you spread your legs for another man," she said.

Having curves is another red flag, as every sentence begins with "From now on," as if we had wronged and were being punished for something beyond our control.

"From now on, you're going to have to sit cross-legged, no

more sitting with legs spread open. And you're going to have to keep an eye on your cleavage every time you sit or get up."

And "From now on, you're not to attend sex education in school," she'd say, in fear that I'd get pregnant out of wedlock.

A part of me wishes that I had Beh's little boy body, for her flat chest and stick figure gets her out of Mâdar's control.

Eating the baked goods is all I'm looking forward to this late afternoon. The same can be said for Alif, as he sits uncomfortably in a corner of the living room jam-packed with middle-aged women from mosque.

Beh whispers in my ear, "Alif looks like Colonel Sanders. Who do you think looks more ridiculous? Alif or Massud's wife and their two dipshit daughters?"

We laugh.

"Do you think Sahar stands a chance at beating me in the poetry competition?" Beh asks. Sahar is Massud's youngest daughter.

"Not a chance," I say. "You probably already know this, but I think your poem is better than the other four contestants."

"Yeah, but I won't be reading that one," she says. She winks and smiles devilishly.

"What'd you mean?" I ask even though I'm not surprised.

"I've been working on another poem . . . a much better one," she says out loud, not caring if Sahar hears her.

I laugh. "And how do you plan to get away with that? The poems have already been selected."

Beh smiles from ear to ear. She says, "So what? This poem will even have the grade twelves talking."

"Does Alif know about all of this?" I ask.

"Of course he does. He's the only one I've read the poem to."

I don't bother to ask her to share it with me. I'm always the last to find out about Beh's master plans.

Finally, du'âs come to an end, a signal for Alif to join Padar in the basement. A ceremony thrown in his honour, and all that's required of him is to make an appearance.

Mâdar signals me to the kitchen to serve tea. Now that she needs my help, she's ready to talk to me.

I stick my head out the kitchen window to catch a whiff of fresh air.

"Get your head out of there and serve the tea before it gets cold," Mâdar tells me. She fills each ceramic teacup to the brim before placing it on the newly purchased tea tray. Not once does she spill a drop of tea.

"Serve this, more's coming. And don't forget to take the apples. Alif was up early picking the finest ones," she says. Our backyard consists of a dozen fruit trees, yet it's the apple tree she takes great pride in.

As tea is being served, music blares out of the speakers. Now that Alif is gone, the women make themselves comfortable by taking their head scarves off. They look different with their hair curled and their ears, necks and wrists covered in jewelry. They've also retouched their makeup and applied more perfume, for the tang is overpowering. My eyes dry and my nose begins to itch, sensitive to the different scents.

"It fucking reeks in here," Beh says.

The women take turns dancing and playing man and coy wife. Some twirl around, some dance bandari, some dance in ways inauthentic and some dance like newcomers to Canada.

Once the women dance themselves to exhaustion, Mâdar grabs a large plastic bowl from the kitchen drawer and sings a traditional song called "Shakoko jân." Based on a beautiful Kandahari woman named Shakoko, the song is about her being desired for her pearly white teeth, jet-black eyes and big house.

Suddenly, Beh and I notice two heads peeping through the window. Beh runs and flings the door open. The women scream and hide as their bodies are exposed. Pretending to close the door behind her, I follow her outside, knowing that it'll be my only chance at getting out of this mehmouni.

"What the hell are you doing?" Beh asks, running toward Ryan and Terry.

"Nothing," says Ryan. He's more scared of Beh than Terry is.

"Stop being a creeper or I'll send my mom after both of you," she says. She looks through the window only to learn that they were eyeing Massud's two daughters. "You want me to tell them that you were jerking off to them?"

I laugh.

"That's not who we were looking at," says Terry.

Alif suddenly appears, relieving them of Beh's bullying. "What are you guys doing here?" he asks them.

Ryan changes the subject. He asks, "What's going on in there?"

"We're throwing a party for Alif," Beh answers.

"How come we're not invited?" asks Terry.

"Yeah, why are there only women in there? What kind of a party is this?" Ryan asks.

"We're honouring Alif's circumcision," Beh answers again.

"What's that?" Ryan asks, confused.

Alif tries to cover Beh's mouth, but she pushes him away, managing to spit out a few words. "It's when they slice the tip of your dick off."

I laugh again, this time louder.

"What?" the twins ask at the same time.

"Is that why you didn't come to school last week?" asks Terry.

For a split second, the brothers think Beh is joking, until they notice the look of distress on Alif's face. The twins fall to the ground, dying from laughter. Me and Beh join them.

"You people are fucking weird," says Terry, as he lets out a snort.

"So where is it?" Ryan asks.

"Where's what?" Alif asks.

"The tip of your dick."

Alif first throws a punch at Ryan and then at Terry.

I grab Alif's arms, fearing that a bigger fight will break loose.

Suddenly, we notice Jonathan coming out of the bushes. He looks at Alif and laughs. Alif tries to break free but I hold his arms tighter.

Padar comes out of hiding. "Party's over. Get inside," he shouts.

*

I search for Firishta after the guests are forced to leave. I look in all the rooms, including the basement and the balcony, thinking Mâdar has tucked the poor creature away.

"Where's Firishta?" I ask. I look over at Padar and he looks away.

"Firishta is missing!" I shout this time.

"It's not missing, I gave it away," Mâdar says.

"What?"

"To Latifa's daughter," she says.

Again, I look over at Padar, who looks unaffected.

"What gave you the right?" I ask Mâdar.

Mâdar busies herself with tidying. I walk right up to Padar. He buries his head deep in his newspaper.

"Why can't you just accept that you're second?" I blurt out to Mâdar, mostly to get Padar's damn attention.

Mâdar stops to face me. With a shaking voice, she asks, "Excuse me?"

"The second wife, the second mâdar —"

Padar slams the newspaper on the coffee table. He shouts, "Shabnam —"

I shake my head at him. "Why are you taking her side? Just yesterday you were saying Firishta stays for me."

He charges at me and says, "Apologize to your mâdar. Right now."

"Are you serious? Why can't she apologize to me for once?"

"You don't get to talk like that to your mâdar," Padar shouts.

"She's not my mâdar — she's my nana andar," I say, because *nana andar* is more debasing than *mâdar andar.*

In all these years, Mâdar has never called me stepdaughter just like I've never called her mâdar andar. But, just because these words weren't exchanged, it doesn't mean that they didn't enter our minds, changing how we look at and treat each other.

Monster, Monster

Nana andar is a monster.

Padar grits his teeth. "Apologize."

"No."

"If you had any idea what she went through for you . . ." Padar says.

"Why are you telling me this? You'd never throw something like this in Alif's or Beh's face," I shout.

"I told her to," Padar suddenly reveals. "It was my idea to give the bird away. I should've never bought it in the first place — it was unfair to your mâdar, Beh and Alif."

I step back. Padar tries to come closer but I push him with my tears, which twirl turbulently out of my eyes. "Stay away from me. Both of you."

In my bedroom, I go to draw the curtains and notice Jonathan from outside my window. He's in his bedroom holding something. When he sees me, he walks over to open his window. He sticks his arm out. A dead bird sits on his palm. I gasp and jump back.

Slowly, I walk back to the window. Jonathan is gone. His bedroom lights are out, the window is shut and the blinds are drawn. *Am I imagining all of this?* Mâdar isn't cruel enough to hurt Firishta, is she?

CHAPTER

NINE

Friday, March 10, 2000

Alif and Beh swing the school doors open and enter as I walk behind them. Beh is more excited than usual — she walks down the hallway, spitting out Lil' Kim's "Queen Bitch" lyrics, as if she's already won the poetry contest.

Mr. "Potato Head" Jackson, Mrs. "Knee Knocker Tits" Milne and Mrs. "Heads for Tits" Lam — nicknames given to them by Alif and Beh — whisper to one another in the corridor as they see the two.

"You watch your language," Mr. Jackson shouts at Beh, revealing his buckteeth.

With mouth wide open and protruding teeth, Beh says, "Good morning to you too." She then asks Mrs. Milne, "You excited for me to win today?"

"Very excited," she says before turning to her colleagues to roll her eyes.

"What makes you think you're going to win?" Mrs. Lam shouts.

"Mr. Harvey says that rhetorical questions aren't meant to be answered," Beh says. She high-fives Alif, who's always encouraging her inappropriate behaviour.

Beh isn't an idiot — she knows the teachers are mocking her, yet she doesn't seem to be bothered. I wish I had an ounce of her courage.

Beh's two nerdy sidekicks — whom she likes to refer to as "Doorknob" and "Doormat" — wait at Beh's locker. They first help Beh with her knapsack and books and then Alif.

"Where to?" Doormat asks them.

"We've got time. Let's say hi first," Alif says.

I head to my locker and watch Beh and Alif walk past different cliques, which the two have nicknamed. Doorknob, who mimics Alif's walk, clears the way as they greet the "Filipino breakdancers," the "Asians that bombard the cafeteria microwave during lunch period," the "Serbs that rule the cafeteria," the "too-cool-for-school South Asians," the "lesbian hippies," the "Persian metrosexuals with plucked eyebrows" and the "white walking boners."

The bell rings and Doorknob and Doormat walk them to their classes.

At 10:00 a.m., the grade twelves are asked to proceed to the gym first.

Mr. Thompson, the principal, waits patiently for the audience to quiet down before starting the event. "Our contestants have been working hard on their poems. We ask that you show your respect by saving your applause for the very end. Cellphones should be turned off and there should be no talking during the presentations. Parents, please wait to take photos after the event is complete," he says.

The audience becomes weary, a sign for Mr. Thompson to move faster. He turns to the panel of judges and smiles. "We have five exceptional judges, all of whom hold a master's in English literature: Mr. Lee, Mrs. Wong, Mr. Chan, Mr. Harvey and Ms. Sandhu. They will be judging contestants based on their writing skills, performance and effort. The winner will be selected to represent our school at the annual 'Poets' Voices Award' in Toronto."

When Mr. Harvey's name is called, the students holler.

Mr. Harvey was voted one of the best teachers in our school because he hardly teaches, barely assigns homework and doesn't complain or punish students for speaking over him. He has a mutual understanding with his students: he doesn't acknowledge their existence, and vice versa.

Rumour has it that early on in his career, Mr. Harvey had passion and drive. But after twenty years of teaching in a school that's poorly funded and lacking caring staff and administration, he's become rusty and unmotivated. He even eats lunch — always a ham and cheese sandwich on plain white bread — alone, in his unorganized and cluttered classroom.

"Please welcome Harinder Gill from grade twelve, Justin Cheng from grade eleven, Sonia Prasad from grade ten, Sahar Elham from grade nine and . . ." Mr. Thompson stops to crack his fingers and his neck before calling out the final contestant. Sounding nervous, he continues, "and Beh Afshar from grade eight."

Massud and his wife stand and cheer as their daughter Sahar is called to the stage. Sahar poses for a photograph before sitting in her seat. I lower my head, not wanting them to recognize me in the crowd.

Whispers grow louder as the audience waits for Beh to walk to the stage. Mr. Thompson looks worried; his face turns red.

Mr. Thompson isn't the only one on edge, so are all the other teachers on the panel.

Beh has been building up to this moment for a while. This morning on our walk to school, Beh said the following about Mr. Thompson: "That old woman's vagina breath won't know what's coming!"

"Just don't get yourself suspended," I replied.

Suddenly, my teacher pulls me aside. "Your sister needs to speak to you. She says it's urgent. She's waiting for you offstage."

I meet Beh, who has just finished crying, and is waiting for me in a dark corner.

"What's the matter?" I ask.

"Mr. Harvey told the class this morning that it's his last day. He's off to Mexico to get married, and then he's going on his honeymoon. We're going to have a substitute teacher for the next three months," she says.

The thought of Mr. Harvey getting married makes me sick, but instead, I say, "This is why you called me?"

"This ruins everything," she cries. "I can't be the talk of the town after being hit with news like this. How could he betray our love?"

"Shut up, Beh. Get yourself together and get out there. You've already embarrassed me enough," I say and then walk away.

Once sitting, I can't stop staring at Mr. Harvey. *Who would marry that?* I don't even know what Beh sees in him. He's old, fat, hairy and the most unattractive teacher at North Hall Secondary. But none of that matters to her because she claims to love him for praising her writing.

When her name is called, she gloomily walks to the front of the stage. She takes a deep breath and speaks into the microphone. "Poo, poop, crap, shit, dump, load. Fecal matter, bowel movement, excrement —" she says.

Laughter strikes. Mr. Thompson jumps off his seat and rushes to the podium. "What are you doing?"

Beh continues, "These are only words, empty words that fail to capture the essence and beauty of life that discharges from my body —"

"Beh, stop. Go to my office right now," Mr. Thompson says even though he can't be heard over the uproar.

"The noises coming out of my asshole is orchestra to my ears. Most people are mesmerized by their reflection in water —"

Mr. Thompson, almost shouting, says, "Parents, staff and students . . . I'm terribly sorry for all of this."

"I, however, am enamoured by the reflection of the beauty emitting out of my asshole as it hits the toilet bowl."

Before Mr. Thompson rushes to snatch the microphone out of her hand, Beh says, "Look, I can't do this anymore. The only thing I care about winning is Mr. Harvey."

Jaws drop. Beh is now being laughed at.

She drops her microphone and stomps her way to Mr. Harvey. She stands a few inches away from him before climbing on top of the judges' table. She takes out a slip of paper and throws it in front of him — at this point, even I'm taken by surprise.

Beh then pushes her hair to the back and pulls her pants down.

I stand up, gasping.

What is she doing? That disease is going to get herself expelled.

She grabs her panties and starts to pull them down. That's when I'm left with no other choice than to flood the gym with my tears.

I'll never forget the screams, the looks of terror and the streaks of blood splattered on the judges' faces. "She's a monster," my graduating class whispered back and forth. Yet, worse than the name-calling was the look on Beh's face: like she'd just been slaughtered. With fiery eyes, I could make out her lips saying, "This wasn't supposed to be about you."

Instantly, I became the "talk of the town," not Beh. I didn't just gain fame from my own grade, but the entire school. Being a monster gained me popularity in almost every school in the district.

Late at night, Alif and I sneak into the basement to read the note she wrote for Mr. Harvey. If Beh were to ever find out, she'd kill us.

Dear Mr. Harvey,

Before you run off to make the biggest mistake of your life, ask yourself this:

CAN YOUR "FIANCE" LIST THE WAYS SHE LOVES YOU IN ABECEDARIAN? Does she even know what *abecedarian* means?

I love your abs that are hidden under folds of skin.

I love your bushy and greasy eyebrows.

I love your crumbs of food that stick to your moustache.

I love your dandruff that rests on your shoulders.

I love your eye goop in the corners of your eyes.

I love your food that gets stuck in between your teeth.

I love your growing belly.

I love your hair poking out of your ears.

I love your intense breath first thing in the morning.

I love your jovial smile that makes me feel warm and fuzzy on the inside.

I love your kissable earlobes.

I love your lint that lives in your belly button.

I love your masculine high-pitched voice.

I love your nipples on a cold morning, erect and poking out of your sweater.

I love your oval-shaped balding head.

I love your permanent pit stains.

I love your quick decision to smell everything before you place it in your mouth.

I love your rubbing of your thighs as you walk.

I love your strands of hair that are attached to the mole on your face.

I love your taste of creme-filled donuts that you jam into your mouth.

I love your urine-smelling trench coat.

I love your voluptuous man boobs.

I love your wide waistline.

I love your xerotic knuckles and fingertips.

I love your yellow-tipped fingernails.

I love your zebra-print scarf that hides your thick neck.

Yours truly,

Beh Afshar.

CHAPTER

TEN

Sunday, May 7, 2000

The average human has about six litres of blood, and long before a person bleeds out, their body goes into shock. Mine doesn't, and it wasn't until a series of exhaustive tests, which left doctors flabbergasted as they were unable to diagnose or treat me, that I began to see myself as a monster.

I have enough bloody tears to cause serious damage to my surroundings. How do I know this? I was four when I had my first blood bath, a memory that will forever be engrained in my mind.

Padar booked the family a motel room that took months to pay back. "We'll take the room with the biggest Jacuzzi and bathtub," he told the woman at the front desk. When we entered our room, Padar slipped my shoes off and placed me in the bathtub. He turned the lever to the stopper and demanded that I cry.

"Cry, my child. Cry with every drop of blood in you," he told me. I cried and cried, never feeling so terrified and empowered at the same time.

"Cool," was the word that came out of Alif's mouth.

I stood on my tippytoes to catch a glimpse of myself in the mirror. Ripples of blood ran down my body, looking like a can of red paint had exploded all over me.

"Faster," Padar said.

I let the tears pour out of me until my blood overflowed, splattering soundlessly onto the tiled bathroom floor.

"Stop," Padar said. He picked me up and placed me in the Jacuzzi. "Continue."

I cried, this time faster, colouring all of me, from the neck down, in red. As the Jacuzzi was filling, Padar began to drain the thick pool of blood from the bathtub. "I think there's more coming," he whispered to Mâdar.

Once I was finally done, Padar asked me, "Is that all?"

I nodded, having filled up the Jacuzzi and bathtub a total of eight times each.

"You have a gift . . . a very special one," he then told me.

Padar always esteemed it, referring to it as his red tears of pearl. Alif and Beh were always fascinated by it. The only person who never really got used to it was Mâdar; she dreaded it. As I got older, my bloody tears increased. I can now control my tears — they can trickle, flood, twirl and erupt, all under my command.

Regardless of the "gift" I have, I don't like to cry. I can't step into a bathtub without thinking back to that day. Sometimes if I look hard enough, I can see my blood swirling down the drain after every bath.

Today, I wish to take another blood bath, with the person who's revolted by it the most, Mâdar.

The closer Mâdar is to dying, the more the guilt of calling her "nana andar" seeps through. I'm ashamed for waiting this long to apologize.

Monster, monster.

I am a monster.

I enter her room and tiptoe into the bathroom. With her back turned to me, Mâdar steps into a half-full tub of lukewarm water. She sits down, extends her legs, closes her eyes and lets her body relax. "Kareem?" she says as she hears me walking closer to her. Eyes still closed, Mâdar begins to untie the top of her hospital gown.

"It's me," I say. When she realizes it's me, she reties the top.

"Where's your padar?" she asks. She turns around and sits up to face me. "He's supposed to give me a bath."

"He'll be back later. I told him I need to speak to you alone," I say.

As Mâdar tries to stand in the tub, I stop her. I step in and sit to face her. "It's best we stay in the tub," I say.

"What's the matter?" she asks.

Immediately, I let my grief pour out in a wave, stopping right at Mâdar's chest — enough to respect her privacy. Even though my blood is mixed with water, the pool of blood is crimson. The heavy flow is warm — like a red thick blanket, it feels soft against my skin. I look into Mâdar's eyes and for once, she doesn't seem to care about the residue of my tears.

"I owe you an apology, something that should've happened a while ago," I say.

Mâdar's face softens. A faint smile sits on her lips.

"You're the greatest mâdar I could ever ask for. I had no right calling you 'nana —'" I try to say before I find Mâdar's fingers pressed against my lips. She does not want to hear those words again, reliving it is too painful for her.

"I forgive you. No mâdar stays upset at their children forever," she says. "We say things we don't mean when we're upset. I'm guilty of that all the time."

"I wasn't just acting out of anger, I wanted to hurt you."

Mâdar takes a deep breath. "I said I forgive you."

She then places both hands on my red cheeks and says, "I'm sorry about Firishta — I didn't mean for it to go that far. I let jealousy and fear of losing you get the best of me."

Mâdar can no longer keep her tears back. I wipe her tears away, she wipes mine.

"My whole life I felt like I had another woman's shoes to fill. I felt like that being married to your padar . . . I didn't want to feel like that with you," she says.

"No one can ever replace you. You're my mâdar. Like you said, blood isn't everything," I say.

"No, it isn't. But, it's your right to want to know more about your blood. I shouldn't have gotten in the way of that."

Under the pool of blood, I extend my arms to her. When our fingers touch, I pull her close and wrap my arms around her. I spread my legs and bring her closer to me. With my chest becoming her pillow, I let a red streak run down her head. It tucks behind her ear before dripping back into our blood bath. I hold her until she's done crying.

CHAPTER

ELEVEN

Tuesday, May 9, 2000

At 6:00 a.m., we're woken up by a bang on our bedroom doors.
We all come running out, knowing exactly what has happened.

Padar's lips tremble. "Your mâdar . . ." he says, not needing to
finish his sentence.

We run out of the house and into the car.

Once in Mâdar's unit, we run past the nurses and hover over
Mâdar's body. Padar is the last to come close. With his first few
steps being the fastest, he stops once he reaches Mâdar's bedside.

Alif has his arms wrapped around Mâdar's neck, Beh has her
hand sitting on her cheek and I'm caressing her hand.

I rest my head on Mâdar's shoulder and watch Padar stand
motionless.

I move to make way for Padar. He sobs uncontrollably.

I take a few steps back and watch. Padar has lost so much —
first Mojda and now Mâdar. I look at Alif and Beh, both who are
equally torn. *Beh is only thirteen.* As the eldest, I don't know

how I'm going to help them cope through all of this. I then look down at my own tears. I too have lost so much.

For the first time, I cannot control my tears. Blood flows down my face like a long red stream. A tear hits the side of Alif's cheek. He uses his fingers to wipe it away.

"Don't make this about you," Beh shouts.

I ignore her. I've been careful with my tears for too long and I don't care anymore. I let the tears pour out, freely.

Blood is on the heels of their shoes, becoming slippery. Alif runs to shut the door.

"You're getting your fucking blood all over her," Alif then says.

Blood runs down Mâdar's leg.

"Make her stop," Beh tells Padar.

Once Mâdar's entire body is covered in blood, Padar speaks. "Shabnam," he says. He carefully makes his way toward me, afraid that I may strike him with the uncontrollable force that lives within me.

"This isn't about me. It never is. I just can't keep it in anymore," I say.

Padar slips. He gets back up, this time walking slowly. "I know, I know —" he tries to say before Beh interrupts.

"I have things I'm keeping inside too. You don't see me dirtying Mâdar's body," she says.

The tears are now coming faster and heavier.

"Quiet, Beh. You're not helping," Padar says.

Padar rests his hands on my face. He says, "You're in pain, I can see that. We've all been through a lot. I'm not going to promise that things will get easier. I'm not even going to promise that

I'll be here for all of you the same way your mâdar was. But what I can promise is to be here and try my best. Cry, you have as much right to do so as we do."

I drop to the floor. I sink to my knees in a puddle of my own blood before taking my hands to my face. I wail.

Padar joins me. He wraps his arms around me until the red mighty river in my eyes finally calms. Waves turn into droplets.

I look up at Beh and Alif and say, "See? There are no tulips, only blood and monstrosity."

Mâdar's body is finally transported in a white plastic body bag. Not until her corpse is wheeled out and put in a hearse, do we realize that she's actually gone.

I wish I were a better daughter. I wish I could take back all the hurt I've caused her. I wish I could take back calling her "nana andar."

"Let's go," Padar whispers, his voice trembling.

We first go home to change our bloody clothes before driving to mosque, where we find Kâkâ Farhad and Khâla Wajma waiting for us. Kâkâ Farhad and Alif help Padar transfer Mâdar's body onto the cushioned, sturdy table placed in the centre of the mor-da shouy khâna.

Padar and Kâkâ Farhad cry in one another's embrace before Alif joins them. Khâla Wajma throws herself in my arms, crying. When she goes to Beh, Beh walks away.

Before the door to the washing room closes, Beh stops Khâla

Wajma from entering. "Take one fucking step closer . . ." she says.

Any other time, Padar would've cursed her; instead, he says, "I think it'd be best if just me and the girls wash Farzana."

The door to the washing room closes, with Khâla Wajma looking at Beh with darting eyes.

The room is white and squeaky clean, exactly how Mâdar would want it.

Padar unzips the plastic body bag. My body shivers at the sight of Mâdar — three hours haven't even passed and any colour on Mâdar's face has faded. Padar reaches for scissors, and in a straight line, he cuts through Mâdar's bloody hospital gown and disposes it and the bag in a garbage can not far from me.

This is my first time seeing Mâdar naked. Her eyes are closed, her hands and feet straightened, her muscles are relaxed and the incision on her head is devastating to see. Her body is cold.

Padar first places a white cloth on Mâdar's private parts. Then, with a cloth tightly wrapped around his hand, he wipes the blood from her body, starting from the head and neck and working his way down to the right and left sides of her body. He does this several times until all the blood is gone.

Padar disposes the cloths and asks Beh to hand him more. This time, he uses the cloth only to wipe Mâdar's private parts. Again, he disposes it.

Now that Mâdar's body is wiped down, the real bath occurs. Mâdar's body is washed three times, and each time, Padar is careful in preventing water from entering Mâdar's mouth and nose. "Bismillâh," Padar repeats over and over.

The first time, the water is mixed with lote tree leaves. The second time, the water is mixed with camphor, and the third time, the water is left untouched, in "its pure state," as Mâdar would say.

Mâdar's body is fragrant, clean and ready to be shrouded. Three white sheets are then used to wrap her body.

When the door opens, Alif comes running in. Padar, Kâkâ Farhad and he gently place Mâdar's body in a wooden box before placing it into the hearse.

We get in the car. Padar drives in silence as he follows the hearse to a cemetery located in the middle of nowhere.

A large hole waits for Mâdar. The men set the box down, right in front of the sheik, who's already arrived. He recites a few prayers for Mâdar as we all gather around.

Once Mâdar is taken out of the box, my heart rips through my chest.

Mâdar is placed in the dirt, with her feet pointing to the qibla. Her body is rested on its right side with her cheek placed on earth and her head resting on a pillow of clay. "Humans are made from dirt. When we die, we go back to that dirt," she'd say whenever tending to her apple tree.

Trying very hard to not fall apart, Alif whispers azân in Mâdar's right ear while Padar places one tasbeh and one mohr close to her body. Layers of heavy stones are then placed over her, topped by three handfuls of dirt by Alif. With hands smeared in dirt, Alif brings them to his face and cries. Beh and I embrace him.

*

When we finally arrive home, I lock myself in the basement. I cry and cry. I float in my pool of blood. My eyes finally cave to sleep. I close them, not caring if I drown.

I sink all the way to the bottom. All is dark.

Suddenly, a force pulls me up. I cough up blood; it even comes out of my nose. I open my eyes to find the pool of blood gone.

A familiar shadow looms near me. It calls out my name, "Shabnam jân."

"Mâdar?" I cry. "Is that you?"

The shadow whirls close to me. A hazy cloud shapes into a woman's silhouette.

It's Mâdar. I think I'm dreaming but I'm not. Everything looks and feels real — her touch, her smell, her essence.

Mâdar lies beside me. Bodies nestled and hairs knotted, the ghost binds her feet with mine. I lift my head and turn to look at her. She brushes a strand of hair from my face before running her hands through my hair. Sweeter than any kiss or caress, her arms tighten around me. She blankets me with her dress, locking out the worries of the world.

"Go back to sleep, my child," she whispers gently into my ears.

PART 3 – I

ALIF

CHAPTER

TWELVE

Sunday, April 2, 2000

Padar runs toward our restaurant as me and Mâdar step out of the car. I haul a bag of groceries behind him. GO HOME is graffitied in big, black, bold letters on the front of the building.

Mâdar runs over to join Padar, who looks to see if Kâkâ Farhad's shop is also vandalized. Nothing. He's relieved and confused at the same time.

Padar places a hand on my shoulder and says, "Alif, fill a bucket with soapy water and bring it outside, along with a few scrubbing pads and cleaning sprays. I'm going to call the police."

Mâdar grips both of his hands. "Kareem, I'm scared," she says.

"Don't be. Stay inside and lock all the doors. We'll clean all of this," he says.

I lug the bags inside, with Mâdar following me.

This isn't the first time we've been hit with racism. "Sand nigger," "terrorist," "shit on a stick" and "Paki" are only some of the names I've been called. Mâdar, especially, is hated on for her hijab. Yet, it's never stung like this before — Canada is our home. Where the fuck are we to go?

I do as I'm told and meet Padar outside. I begin to scrub as Padar gives the dispatcher more information.

He gets off his phone and joins me. With a hunch in our shoulders, we scrub until the tips of our fingers crack and our nails become jagged.

I sigh. "This isn't working," I tell him.

"Keep trying," he says as he stands up to head inside. "I'm going to grab more dish soap and scrubbies."

I follow him, to wash the chemicals off my hand.

Mâdar hasn't moved a hair; she hasn't even taken her jacket off. She stands in the kitchen looking blank.

Padar looks at her disappointingly. "You haven't been standing there the entire time, have you? We're opening in a few hours," he says.

"Have you lost your mind? We can't be open today," Mâdar says.

"Why not?" Padar asks.

"We need a few days off to figure things out. The police aren't even here yet," Mâdar says.

"The police will be here. There's nothing to figure out. All that matters is our reaction. Whoever did this is trying to scare us, trying to push us out — they're a bunch of cowards hiding behind their markings on a wall. The only way to fight back is by staying put," Padar says.

Mâdar is nearly in tears. "For once, just listen to me. Let's take a few days off —" she tries to say.

"We can't afford to take a few days off," Padar shouts. "Don't let two words scare you."

I wash my hands and dry them, preparing myself for the argument that's about to break loose.

"Are you not worried for the children?" Mâdar then asks.

"Do you see anyone that's hurt?" Padar asks.

Suddenly, voices are heard from outside. "That's probably the police," Padar says.

Padar curses once outside. He brushes his hand through his hair and kicks the wall, hard. Mâdar and I rush outside. A dozen or so eggs have been thrown at the wall. I make two fists and try to run after the group of boys who run off, laughing.

Mâdar grabs me by the collar. "You trying to get yourself hurt? Get inside!" she shouts.

Padar comes after me. He speaks to me as if nothing had just happened. "Why are you inside? Get back out there and help me. We have a bigger mess to clean now."

Mâdar grabs my arm and says, "He's not going anywhere."

I hate it when they do this. I hate it when they try to get me involved. I look down and keep my lips sealed.

"So we're just supposed to hide in here all day?" Padar asks her as he shoves a spray in my hand and pulls me out of her clasp. He then looks at me and says, "You, out of all people, know not to give into fear. If we give in today then where does that leave us tomorrow?"

"Kareem, stop," Mâdar begs.

Padar now tries to reason with Mâdar. He says, "Sure, we can change the music, change our uniforms and bring in tables and chairs, but what kind of example would we be making for our children? They need to learn to take pride in their culture, not be ashamed of it. Aren't you the one that's always saying our children are forgetting their roots?"

"This isn't about fear or being ashamed of who we are. This is about our children's safety," Mâdar says.

"Fine, then let's wait until the police get here," Padar says.

"The police don't care about us, Kareem. If they did, they would've been here by now."

"It hasn't even been that long. They'll be here. I promise," Padar says.

"Then you can keep waiting for them. I'm taking Alif home with me," Mâdar says.

Padar slams his fists on the kitchen countertop. "You don't think Farhad went through this when he first opened up Bismillâh Halal Market?" he says.

Mâdar ignores him. She's already made up her mind.

Padar takes a deep breath. Once in a calmer state, he takes a different approach. "Remember when we first came to Canada? We didn't have a penny in the bank. I don't want that for our children, they shouldn't have to taste poverty. Maybe one day we can buy a house. We'd finally stop renting. We could even go to Mecca as a family," he says.

"Stop it," Mâdar cries. She pushes him away. "I can't listen to any more of your false promises. This place is a curse, it's done nothing but drive us into debt. We haven't even been open for a week and already the children are falling behind in school. I say we just shut down."

Padar looks at me in a final attempt to get me involved. Instead, I walk to the closet, grab the broom and start sweeping the already clean floors.

He then distances himself from the both of us and laughs hysterically. "Is this some joke to you? Our entire life savings have been invested in this business. You're overreacting."

"We were just egged, Kareem, and that's only the beginning of it. It'll only get worse. Not even Farhad had to deal with any of this," Mâdar says.

Mâdar turns around when, suddenly, Padar says, "Your prayers must've been answered?"

"Excuse me?" she says.

Padar gets incredibly close to Mâdar, so close that it worries me.

"You've been waiting for something like this to happen for a long time so that you can turn your back on me," he says.

"You're crazy. I don't have time for this. Alif, grab your things and let's go," Mâdar says.

She walks away from Padar, yet it doesn't stop him from coming close to her again.

"Everyday you come in here with a long face, acting like your hands and feet are tied together. You never wanted to be here from the very beginning," he says.

"How dare you? I'm here working all day like a dog," Mâdar shouts.

"I'm here working like a dog too. We're doing this together, for our family," he says.

The two speaking about working like dogs reminds me of a joke Beh shared one evening over dinner. "When you search

Afghan in the dictionary, two meanings show up," Beh said. She then looked at me courageously. "People from Afghanistan and a type of dog."

We both laughed.

"Why is that so funny?" Padar asked, eagerly waiting for a rational explanation.

"Because I can't tell the difference between a dog and an Afghan," Beh said.

Mâdar and Padar fit perfectly into the second definition. I take pity on them — both are equally miserable, treating each other terribly. Is it possible to love and hate your parents at the same time? Because lately, that's how I've been feeling.

Padar's veins are now bulging out of his neck and his eyes are red.

Mâdar stoops to his level. "Stop pretending that you're doing this for the family then," she says.

Padar pulls on his hair and shouts, "Then who? Then who is this all for?"

"For you! It's always been about you. All you've ever thought about was yourself. This 'business' was another way for you to prove yourself to Farhad. The children are constantly making sacrifices so that you can compete with your brother. Spare the family from all of this headache and just accept that you've lost to him, again," Mâdar says. She takes a mixing bowl from the sink and throws it on the floor.

"You'd like that, wouldn't you, to see me be the laughing-stock?" Padar asks.

"See?" Mâdar says, now laughing. "Everything has always been about you and protecting your honour!"

"I don't need you. Get the hell out of here," Padar then says. He pushes her out of his way.

"Good. Let's go, Alif," she says, grabbing her purse before throwing my hoodie at me. "Your padar can manage on his own."

"Where do you think you're taking him?" Padar asks. He rushes toward me and pulls me to him.

"He's coming with me," Mâdar says. She grabs me by the other arm.

"No, he's not," he says.

I push both of their arms away before they tear my fucking limbs off. *This isn't no damn tug-of-war.* I slip my hoodie on and start heading out the back door.

"Alif, you leave that door . . ." Padar threatens.

"What? What will you do to him, Kareem?" Mâdar asks.

"Don't turn your back on me, son," he cries.

"Let him go home, Kareem. Let him spend his weekends home, like every other child," Mâdar says.

"He's not a child. Let him take some responsibility."

"He is a child and he's my son. I get to say what he can and can't do," Mâdar says.

"Your son?" Padar says, now grabbing Mâdar tightly by the arm.

They fight over me as if I'm property. Depending on the severity of their fight, one second I'm my mâdar's son and the next, I'm my padar's.

As the only son, there are things I've heard and seen that neither Beh nor Shabnam has. A sixteen-year-old boy my age is supposed to be out and about, not watching over his parents during every argument. Whenever these two jump down each other's throats, I'm obliged to lend my ears to them. I'm told multiple versions until truth becomes hazy and every detail turns into a lie. Padar will try to turn me against Mâdar, and vice versa. And, every time, their words cause further separation in the family. Beh always sides with Mâdar and Shabnam always sides with Padar.

"Get away from me," Mâdar says. She slaps him hard; I can see her fingerprints on his face.

Padar pushes Mâdar with all his might, causing her to fall down. Her legs fumble over the mixing bowl before her head hits the cold tiles, hard.

Like an electric shock running through her, Mâdar violently jerks. Her muscles are stiff; her face is flushed and twitches.

I freeze as I watch Padar drop to his knees to shake Mâdar. "Get up," he says. He slaps her a few times, yet no response.

Mâdar is out. Drool hangs down the corner of her mouth.

Minutes later, Mâdar stands up and walks out the door. I follow her.

Padar spends the rest of his day waiting for the police, who never show up. A part of me wished they'd walked in to see Padar push Mâdar.

A part of me wished that I was like the white kids in school and talked — white kids report on their parents to social services, white kids threaten to call the police on their parents. Us coloured kids, we're too scared to talk because we don't want to end up like the ones next door living under Mr. and Mrs. O'Connors' "foster care" — especially Jonathan, who's been with the O'Connors the longest.

So why didn't I just call the police myself to report Padar? Because, let's face it, I'm not white. I'm brown and I've seen what happens to us kids. We turn into junkies, get adopted by some privileged white family, mysteriously disappear or run away and end up dead in some ditch. The same goes for Mâdar — she knows that an Afghan woman with children would be old news to a single man.

CHAPTER
THIRTEEN

Saturday, April 8, 2000

We sit in Mâdar's hospital room with the door shut. Mâdar is looking out the window, Padar is looking at the wall, Shabnam and Beh are looking at Mâdar, and I'm standing back, watching everyone.

Today is Mâdar's third day in the hospital after her fall in the shower. Now that Mâdar's diagnosis is known, we're finally able to spend some time with her, knowing that she won't be taken for more testing.

"Beh?" Mâdar suddenly says.

Beh looks up at her, teary-eyed.

"That's not why I slipped," Mâdar says before she extends her arms out to hold Beh. Beh throws herself in her embrace and sobs. "I don't want you blaming yourself, do you understand?"

Beh blows her nose into a tissue as Mâdar places a hand on her cheek.

"I would've slipped even if you didn't come into the bathroom. See my fall as a good thing. I would've never had the seizures or known about the tumour. You heard the doctor — this hospital has the best neurosurgeons and they're going to do everything to remove it," Mâdar says.

Mâdar looks up at me and Shabnam and smiles. We smile back. When my eyes land on Beh, they begin to water.

I'm far more guilty than Beh is. As the only son, I failed in protecting my mâdar. If only my sisters knew that I'd witnessed Mâdar's first seizure episode and chosen not to do or say anything. If I wasn't a damn coward then maybe Mâdar's tumour would've been caught earlier.

Now, Mâdar's tumour has spread. I don't understand how she puts her trust in the medical team — or Allah, for that matter — when we've already been told that Mâdar has approximately three months to live.

We're all to blame, actually. Mâdar's body had been crying for help for quite some time. The headaches, the double vision and the spasms all make sense now.

Back then, they didn't.

Then, we dismissed them as stress related.

"What were you going to tell me anyway?" Mâdar asks.

"It was nothing. I don't even remember," Beh cries.

"It'll come back to you, and when it does, I want to hear it," Mâdar says.

I look over at Padar, hoping that he'll stop Beh from blaming herself by admitting that the shower incident wasn't the initial sign of Mâdar's spreading tumour. Instead, he remains tight-lipped. I then look down at myself. I too cannot bring myself to relieve my sister.

I feel sick to my stomach. My entire flesh stings. *I'm just like Padar.*

Monster, monster.

I am a monster.

Padar is aware of all the stereotypes being an Afghan carries — "wife beater," "slave owner" and "sultan's harem," to only name a few. "Don't ever be a stereotype, son," Padar would always remind me. He wanted me to grow into a man "that would give Afghan men a better name."

"A true man doesn't raise his voice or his hand on a woman" was more bullshit that came out of his mouth. But what Padar needs to hear is that he, too, is becoming a stereotype. I wonder if he used to beat his half-Kandahari and half-Hazara wife too, or if his abusive hands are only reserved for my mâdar?

Mâdar is also a stereotypical Afghan woman, choosing to stay quiet. Or does she think this is something that just happens in a marriage? Both Mâdar and Padar's favourite explanation is "This is marriage. This is what married couples do." Yet somehow, I'm not mad at her for being a stereotype. She's a victim. She has more to lose than Padar.

For once, I wish I was a stereotype. I wish I took the role of the eldest son more seriously and protected my mâdar.

I walk up to Mâdar and cuddle up to her. She slowly drifts to sleep. I wipe the vomit on her mouth before running my fingers down her face. I look at Padar and whisper, "I hate you," loud enough that only he can hear.

CHAPTER

FOURTEEN

Sunday, May 14, 2000

I eat breakfast in front of a blank television screen. I tap my fork on the edge of the plate as I think of how much Mâdar would've nagged in my ear for eating in the living room — if only she knew that I've been doing this for the past five days.

I've also missed five days of school, five days of work at the Afghan Nomad and five days of tedious exchanges with Padar.

My hate for Padar multiplies each passing day, and at this rate, I don't think I can ever forgive him for putting his hands on my mâdar.

Beh and Shabnam have also been absent from school and the restaurant. When your mâdar passes, you become the saddest children in the world — you become Afghan nomads, having no sense of home.

Even our sadistic schoolteachers feel sorry for us. "Take all the time you need," I was told by Mr. Deed, the school counsellor, over the phone.

Padar, especially, doesn't have the balls to ask for our help at the restaurant. Every day, he goes to work and comes home alone.

"I still have mouths to feed," I overheard him tell his brother one evening.

"Your children need you at home more than anything," Kâkâ Farhad said.

It's undeniable that Padar is hiding behind his work. From the smell of his uniform coming straight out of the dryer every morning, one would never know that Padar is in mourning. I laugh to myself at the promise he made to us when Mâdar passed: "I'm not going to promise that things will get easier. I'm not even going to promise that I'll be here for all of you the same way your mâdar was. But what I can promise is to be here and try my best."

Suddenly, the doorbell rings. Not until Beh yells at me to get the door, do I move.

I open the door at the second ring.

A man and a woman wait outside. The man is fair-skinned and wears his hair combed back. The woman wears a long white trench coat and bright red lipstick.

"We don't believe in God," I tell them, assuming they're Jehovah's Witnesses.

The man laughs. He holds the door open. "You must be Alif," he tells me.

"Yeah and who are you?" I ask.

"I'm Daoud and this is my wife, Yalda," he says, with an Australian accent.

Yalda sticks her hand out, waiting for me to shake it. "Daoud was your mâdar jân's cousin," she says. Seeing that there's no

144

warm welcome, she tucks her hand back into her pocket.

"What?" I ask.

Shabnam and Beh run down the stairs. "Who are you talking to?" Shabnam asks.

"Mâdar didn't have any cousins," I tell the couple.

"What's going on?" Shabnam asks me before turning to the strangers for answers.

"Salâm. Nice to meet you. I'm Daoud and my wife is Yalda. I'm Farzana's cousin. My wife grew up with your mâdar jân under the same roof. That's actually how we met," he says as he looks at his wife and smiles. "We're sorry for your loss. We flew out the second we heard. I know this may seem strange to you, but if you let us in, we can explain everything."

"You knew my mâdar?" Beh asks. There's excitement in her voice.

"Yes, and you must be Beh?" Daoud asks.

Beh nods.

"And you're Shabnam?" Yalda then adds. She shakes Shabnam's hand and then Beh's.

"Wait. How'd you know Mâdar passed?" I ask.

"Wajma jân told us," Yalda says.

Shabnam pushes me out of the way. "Come on in. I'll call Padar and let him know you're here," she says.

"No, please, we're just passing by. We don't plan to stay for long," Daoud says.

Am I the only one who finds this odd? A man and a woman come all the way from Australia to pay their respects to us and not to Padar? What's gotten into my sisters — where's their sense?

Daoud and Yalda enter with their shoes on, plodding on the floors that Mâdar used to pray on.

Shabnam directs them to the living room. The bedsheets and plastic covers on our furniture haven't been removed, something that would've ticked Mâdar off in front of guests.

We take a seat across from them.

"I'm terribly sorry. Khodâ biamorz. Your mâdar's passing is a loss to us all. We're sorry that this is how we have to meet. We'd like to first give our fâtiha, if you don't mind," Daoud says.

The couple bring their hands together to say a few du'âs.

We sit together in silence for a brief moment. Everyone looks down, except for Yalda, who scans her surroundings.

The azân goes off the clock. I hit the button to stop it, imagining Mâdar pulling on my ear for doing so.

"I'm not surprised the azân just went off. Your mâdar jân was always a devout woman," Yalda says.

They seem to know a lot about Mâdar, yet their names have never been mentioned once. Why am I the only one bothered by this? Why did they wait to visit until Mâdar passed away?

They try to bore us with small talk, which only Shabnam has the decency to reply to. Seeing that Beh and I are becoming anxious and impatient, Daoud tries to intrigue us. "Did Farzana jân ever mention that we knew two children with your names?" he asks.

Beh's eyes light up. She's always craving a good story.

"Alif and his sister, Beh, were well-known orphans in Kabul," Daoud says. "Both were skilled in goudi parân. Their kite-flying techniques brought a lot of wealth to their orphanage."

"I always thought we were named after the alphabet," Beh says, looking at me.

Beh wants to know more, but I stop her. "Yes, I knew," I say.

Beh's eyes dart at me, fully aware that I'm lying.

Yalda then pulls a wooden box from her purse. "I have a few photos of your mâdar jân that I'd like to show you," she says.

Inside the box is a worn-out photo album. "Farzana jân and I shared some great memories," she begins, handing Shabnam the album. "She was very dear to my heart."

Shabnam flips through the pages of the album, looking over each photograph with care and curiosity. Beh huddles around her and looks eagerly at the photos.

"She was so beautiful," Shabnam says.

"Yes, she was," Yalda says, smiling. She is now less tense, her shoulders look relaxed. "She had a great sense of fashion too. I'd always sneak into her room and borrow her dresses."

"Who's that?" Beh asks, pointing at the man and woman sitting beside Mâdar.

Shabnam gasps. "Is that Bibi jân and Bâba jân?"

Daoud nods. Shabnam and Beh look in amazement at our grandparents, as none of us have seen a photograph of our grandparents from either side. Mâdar and Padar came to Canada with nothing but stories, lies and secrets.

Daoud explains each photograph as I pretend to take no interest. I study him instead. With his brand name polished shoes, gold watch and plucked eyebrows, he appears too condescending to give a damn about any of us. I then turn to study Yalda, but she's already beaten me to it. She looks at me like she's looking for something.

Yalda then holds the album up to my face. "Why don't you take a look?" she says.

I flip through the album. Most of the photographs are scratched, stained and old. I look at Mâdar and Yalda on horse-back, on hikes and on dance floors. In every image, there appeared a smile — a smile so radiant, a smile I've never seen on Mâdar's face before. *What happened to that smile? Did Padar kill that smile?*

I continue to search for this mysterious woman through the pieces of her past. *Who is this woman? Why is she unfamiliar? Distant?* In every picture, Mâdar's legs and arms are exposed and her hair reaches down to her back. One photo, especially, draws me. I stop to stare at it. I hold back my tears as I see Mâdar in a beautiful, billowy dress. Her hair is curled down to her shoulders and her eyes are beaming.

"I see a lot of you in your mâdar," Yalda suddenly tells me.

I don't respond. Instead, I take the picture out of its compart-ment and bring it close to my face.

"Go ahead, Alif jân, keep that one. In fact, why don't you all choose a picture to keep?" Yalda says.

"Mâdar never mentioned you. Why?" I finally ask.

Daoud looks at Yalda for approval before answering. He says, "We separated ways, like most Afghans who fled the country did when the Soviets invaded. Farzana jân fled to Iran and we fled to Pakistan. We didn't even know she was alive until she moved to Canada."

"And Bibi jân and Bâba jân? What happened to them?" Beh asks, finally her senses kicking in.

"They didn't make it to Iran," Daoud says. He appears tense.

"So all this time you kept in touch with Khâla Wajma but not your own cousin?" I ask Daoud.

Yalda jumps in. "This is our first time hearing that your mâdar jân never spoke of us. We did speak, but over the years, we just drifted."

Now, I'm enraged. I'm sick and tired of death bringing estranged families together. "You already missed Mâdar's funeral," I say.

"We know, and we're sorry," Daoud says.

Yalda ends the visit by handing over a slip of paper to me. "Thank you for letting us in your home. We don't plan to stay in Vancouver for long, but if you wish to meet up in the next few days or so, you can call the top number. On the bottom is our home address and number in Australia, if ever you wish to speak. It was nice to finally meet all of you, but we've got to get going. Please send your padar jân our love. Zindagi sarâyetan bâsha."

And just like that, they are gone, leaving me with a lot of questions and suspicions.

Over dinner, before Shabnam gets the chance to spill the beans on Yalda and Daoud, I finally break my silence with Padar.

"Why didn't you and Mâdar ever mention Yalda and Daoud to us?" I blurt out.

Padar looks up at me. He wipes his mouth and takes a big gulp of water. He asks, "Who told you about Yalda and Daoud?"

"No one. They were here today."

Padar looks at Shabnam. "Why didn't anyone tell me?" he asks. There's anger in his tone, he doesn't even try to hide it.

"Because then you would've chosen to stay home with us?" I shout. I push my plate away and storm off.

Later that evening, when everyone is in bed, I eavesdrop on Padar.

He first shuffles through the kitchen cupboards and takes several pills before picking up the telephone.

I tiptoe closer to him and hide by the stairs.

He's talking to Kâkâ Farhad. He does not greet him. He gets straight to the point. "Who contacted Yalda and Daoud?" he says.

He remains silent as he listens to Kâkâ Farhad. I move closer, yet I still cannot make out what Kâkâ Farhad is saying.

"You tell your wife that if she's trying to scare me, it's not working," Padar says and hangs up.

CHAPTER

FIFTEEN

Thursday, June 15, 2000

"This is all my fault," Beh shouted the night Padar passed away from falling down the attic stairs.

Beh was taken in for questioning by the police. Even though she gave me and Shabnam a more detailed account of what had happened that evening, my gut tells me that there's a lot she isn't telling.

According to Beh, she was woken up in the dead of night by Mâdar's ghost. "Wake up," the ghost shouted in her ear.

Once she was awake, a strong smell reached her and led her to the attic. There, she found Padar speaking to himself. "He can't know," Padar was saying.

Not sleeping or bathing since Daoud and Yalda's visit, Padar had smelled like a corpse.

Beh placed her hand on Padar's shoulder and brought his face close to hers.

Padar, with a flashlight in his hand, was pale and sweating, yet cold to the touch. "What's wrong?" Beh asked him.

And from this point forward, I'm certain Beh is keeping things from me.

Padar was apologizing to her. He said, "I have to break my promise to you or he'll know."

When I asked Beh about this promise, she said she didn't know what he was talking about.

Beh then asked Padar who he was speaking to. He pointed his light at the corner of the attic and said, "The monster."

"You're scaring me, Padar. There's nothing there," Beh said.

"You think I'm crazy, don't you?" Padar then asked her.

"No, I think you're tired. Please let me take you to bed," she said.

Padar refused to move. He rose and started to tidy the attic.

"Why are you here?" Beh asked.

Padar shook his head. "I couldn't sleep. I keep waking up from the same dream," he said.

"What dream?"

Padar looked again in the corner of the room and whispered, "About the monster. She keeps calling me to the attic, threatening to drop the baby if I don't listen to her."

"A baby?" she asked.

"Yes," he said. His lips began to tremble. "Alif . . . as a baby."

"You had a nightmare, Padar. Alif is safe and sound in bed. We can even go and check on him."

"He won't even talk to me anymore," he said as Beh helped him walk down the stairs.

Before Beh tucked Padar in bed, he reached to his bedside table and swallowed two sleeping pills.

"How many of these have you taken?" Beh asked him.

Padar didn't respond. Instead, half asleep, he asked her to stay with him until he fell asleep.

She agreed. She slipped her fingers in his hand and watched him fall asleep before she went back to her bedroom.

Later that night, Padar must've had the same dream because he went back up to the attic.

We all woke up to my name being screamed, followed by a loud thump.

Beh was the first one at the bottom of the stairs, frozen and looking down at Padar's body. Shabnam and I came next. One look and Shabnam screamed. "Call an ambulance," she shouted.

Cops and paramedics rushed to the scene and drew a crowd of rubberneckers. Wrapped in blankets, our neighbours watched from afar — even the O'Connors were there for the show. A look of malice was exchanged as my eyes met Jonathan's. I ran down the front doorstep to meet him. I pushed past the crowd and just like that, Jonathan was gone.

I stood and watched as police officers dragged Beh outside. "This is all my fault," she shouted, over and over.

What was she hiding?

What promise was Padar breaking? And why was Padar having nightmares about me?

CHAPTER

SIXTEEN

Saturday, June 17, 2000

Early in the morning, I sneak out of emergency foster care and take the bus. The bus drives past the Afghan Nomad. I turn away in disgust. I hate that place and everything it represents. Padar made sure we never took a damn break from that shithole. He nearly killed Mâdar from exhaustion, asking her to perfect her dishes for him months before the restaurant even opened. But it wasn't until Mâdar had her first seizure there that I really began to despise the family business. Padar was an idiot to think that I'd want to run the business after they passed. *Fuck being a golden eagle.*

Mâdar and Padar had my entire fate mapped out, unlike their two daughters, who are considered "guests" in their parents' home until they're passed on to their husbands. Being the only son I was expected to wed, have children and then offer a nursing home residence for my parents under my roof.

I hop off the bus and walk to our home.

I climb over the fence and stop at Mâdar's apple tree. I choke up as I remember planting the tree with Mâdar.

"We take for granted the beauty that surrounds us. We spend so much time worrying about ourselves that we neglect to take care of Allah's other creations," she told six-year-old me.

To Mâdar, apple trees were divine spirits. Some early mornings, I'd catch Mâdar in our yard, pressing her ear up against the tree as if the tree was speaking to her.

"What's so special about them?" I asked her.

"They're incredibly special. Every living being depends on trees," she said as she took my hands and placed them on the trunk. I ran my fingers up and down the peeling bark.

"You are no different from this tree," Mâdar said. She brought my hands to her face and blew the bark away. I looked in wonderment as the pieces danced in the wind and fell to the ground.

I listened attentively as my hands were placed on her stomach. She said, "Like a tree, we, too, begin as a seed. You were once a seed spreading out your roots in my belly."

Mâdar grabbed a fistful of soil and kissed it. "Promise me that when you get older, you'll take good care of this tree. Be good to the tree and the tree will produce big delicious apples for you."

"I promise."

I watched Mâdar pat the soil down before helping her water it. She smeared dirt on the tip of my nose and said, "Never forget your roots. Never forget your seed. Never forget the trees. Listen to them and they will guide you."

As I sit under that tree, I look up at the home I made memories

in. It's now taped off with a yellow sash that says POLICE LINE —
DO NOT CROSS.

I take a rock and throw it through a window. I climb up the
awning and break the remaining pieces of glass in the window
with my fist and elbow. Once inside, I make my way down into
the basement.

I sit back and reminisce. It hurts to think about it all. After
Mâdar passed, I hated Padar. I wanted him gone — dead, even.
And now that he is, I'd do anything to have him here by my side.
I close my eyes and relive the evening of Padar's tumble down the
stairs. I hear the sirens, I feel the coldness of my hands as they
clamped over my ears, and I remember the darkness as I closed
my eyes and buried my head in between my legs.

I pull out the pocket knife Kâkâ Farhad gave me the day I quit
Bismillâh Halal Market. "This is one of my favourite knives. It's
never let me down. I want you to have it," he said as I ripped open
the wrapping paper.

The cold blade is sharp. I press the tip of my finger on the end
of the blade and move my finger forward. A small trickle of blood
appears.

I slit both wrists and lay my head on the floor. I let my eyes drift.

Suddenly, a gust of wind enters. I sit up. A cloud appears before me, causing me to choke and suffocate. My eyes sting and
a cold chill runs up and down my spine. The cloud swirls until
it takes the shape of a human body. Still not in focus, it glides
closer and closer to me. It has pallid, translucent fingers and long
black hair.

I rub my eyes and find Mâdar's ghost sitting right next to me.

She's wearing that same billowy dress from Yalda's photograph of her.

My breathing slows as the ghost kneels close to me. It sweeps its hand over my finger, sending a tingly sensation down my arms and hands. I lift them to my face — the blood is gone and the cuts have closed.

I spread my arms out to touch her but she disappears.

"Come back," I shout.

I make another cut in my finger and wait for Mâdar to reappear, but she doesn't.

I then make cuts all over my arms, each gash deeper than the one before.

Mâdar's ghost finally reappears. She cups her hands, catches my blood and throws it into the air. My blood metamorphoses into a thousand red specks. Suddenly, a realization occurs to me.

Monster, monster

Mâdar's a monster.

"Wait a minute . . . why didn't you stop Padar from dying?" I ask, waving the knife at her.

Again, the ghost vanishes.

I head straight for the shed. I kick the door open, grab a rope and run back inside the house. I wrap a noose around a joist.

"Answer me," I threaten.

The ghost does not show herself. Standing on a chair, I wrap the rope around my neck. With my left foot, I kick the chair over and fall down. My toes point down and the rope chafes my neck. I let my body float as it rocks back and forth.

Mâdar doesn't appear and a big part of me doesn't care.

I choke. My eyes roll to the back of my head when, suddenly, the rope splits in half, causing my body to slam to the floor.

My body aches, but I stand up. This time, I look the ghost straight in the eye and cry, "Why didn't you stop Padar?"

Legs trembling, I run back out to the shed again and set the entire place on fire.

"Why?" I shout over and over again as I watch the flames lick the ceiling.

The roof collapses. Illuminating brighter than any ember, the fire screams upon my skin.

Mâdar spreads her arms out. A current electrifies through her fingertips; it sends off a blinding light. An ice ball catapults at me and extinguishes the fire.

Not even setting myself on fire will get her to answer me.

I let out a loud scream before falling to the ground.

Why won't she let me die?

I grab the biggest axe I can get my hands on and rush out, this time trying to kill something of hers.

With my first swing, I make a deep groove in the trunk of her tree. Her words enter my ears, "Promise me that when you get older, you'll take good care of this tree. Be good to the tree and the tree will produce big delicious apples for you."

I try to pull the axe out, but it won't give. I see Ryan and Terry peering over the fence. Finally, I clench tightly onto the axe and grunt loudly. I pull and pull until the axe falls down, right in front of my feet.

I take several more swings, with each becoming feebler. Again, her words force their way through: "Every time a tree is cut, the heavens shake. The clouds part and the earth beneath our feet separates. We owe our lives to the trees."

"I wouldn't do that if I were you," says a voice from over the fence.

I look over and find Jonathan sitting on his back porch step, like he always does. *The fucker speaks.*

He bites into an apple and says, "Then whose apples am I going to eat?"

I look closer; to his left are more apples.

I form two tightly closed fists. "What the fuck do you think you're doing?"

Jonathan continues biting into the apple, this time louder. Chewing with his mouth wide open, he then spits it out, with a gob of phlegm. He holds the half-eaten apple up to his face and throws it on his lawn.

I run next door and kick the O'Connors' fence open. Ryan and Terry come out of hiding and cower behind Jonathan's fence. I run over to Jonathan and stop once I'm a few inches away from him. He laughs.

Nothing scares this fucker. I take a good look at him as he stares me straight in the eye. His nose is the biggest part of his face and his long greasy hair hasn't seen a bar of soap in days.

"Give them to me," I say.

"You want it?" he asks as he grabs another apple, takes a bite and spits it in my face. "Come and get it."

I throw one punch after the other until Jonathan's nose is covered in blood.

Jonathan doesn't fight back. His smirk is the only form of defence that he needs.

Mr. and Mrs. O'Connors at long last appear, pretending to be concerned for him.

"Get off my property, Paki, or I call the cops," Mr. O'Connors says after noticing that the fence door is broken.

The smirk remains on Jonathan's face, even after I walk away.

I return to Mâdar's tree. My body is doused in sweat as each swing drains the life out of me. My arms shake.

I let myself fall down on the yellow grass. I'm light-headed and the sun is shining directly on me. My vision blurs, my breathing turns into panting and my throat is dry. I stick my tongue out to let a drop of sweat hit my parched tongue.

I rise again; my legs wobble. I stand tall before I pull the axe out of the tree. I take another swing when suddenly the gate flings open. Jonathan enters and closes the gate behind him and Ryan and Terry, who come running. He's holding an axe in his hand, an axe much greater in size than the one I have.

The closer he gets to me, the taller he appears.

The Alif from a week ago would be pissing himself right now. The Alif from a week ago would be begging for mercy now. The Alif from a week ago would run away like a coward. But I'm a different Alif today. I want him to strike me; I want him to slaughter me.

I drop my axe to the ground before dropping to my knees. I spread my arms out and completely surrender myself to him. "Do it!" I scream. "Whatcha waiting for?"

Jonathan rushes toward me and stops. We look at each other. I see pain and loss in his eyes. We all have our stories — his is probably far worse. Tears gather in the corners of his eyes. He swings his axe high in the air and strikes right at the tree. He doesn't stop; each swing is mightier than the one before. He growls. His strength is raw and impeccable. With each strike and each dent in the tree, he becomes more alive. I watch him for some time before I pick up my axe and join him. Together we chop the tree down.

Jonathan finally drops his axe and looks up at the sky. When his glance turns to me, the tears start falling.

"We're going to be okay," he tells me in Dari.

My heart pierces. All this time, I thought us Afghan kids don't end up in foster care. We kept our mouths shut and our parents put their hatreds aside to remain as a family for the children. How did he end up here?

"You're not —" I stutter.

"No, I'm not an Indian. I'm Hazara."

CHAPTER
SEVENTEEN

Sunday, June 18, 2000

We're in a suffocating room with Alice, our social worker. She flips through her notebook. "Your uncle, Farhad, has already reached out to me. I've sat down to meet him and his family, and they've expressed that they wish to have you all live with them. This would mean that your uncle would be your legal guardian and that you'd be living under his care until you are all of legal age," she says.

Next, with elbows on the table and hands folded, she says, "And there's no need to worry — your uncle would be financially assisted so that you're all properly taken care of."

Great, because that's exactly what we're worried about — being a fucking financial burden.

She begins to jot a few notes down. "Personally, I think this is the best option. It's my job to ensure that children in similar situations are placed under the care of family and near relatives first before reaching out to distant relatives and family friends," she says.

"We don't have distant relatives or family friends," Beh says, suddenly crying.

Shabnam places a hand on Beh's shoulder.

"We wouldn't need to worry about that in your situation," Alice tells her. She's a lot more sympathetic today than she was the night she placed us in emergency foster care.

Beh's crying worsens. "What if —" she asks. "What if we had no one?"

"Then we'd search for a suitable home," Alice says.

"Together? All three of us?" Beh asks.

Alice nods. "Of course. We never separate siblings."

She closes her notebook and leans in closer. She looks us all in the eye. "I can't even imagine what you're all going through. Even though your relations with your uncle and his family are close, it's still a great change and takes a lot of adjusting —"

Beh cuts her off. "No," she shouts.

Alice sits back, giving Beh time to cool down.

Beh is now hysterical. "No, we can't stay with them. I won't do it," she says.

Alice waits for Beh's tears to stop before she asks, "Is there a reason why?"

Beh shakes her head, refusing to reply.

Again, the sympathy comes in. "I understand," Alice begins, "this has all happened too fast —"

This time, I interrupt her. "We're gonna need a word with our sister."

Alice places her notebook in her briefcase and rises. "Of course. Take your time. I'm just outside, let me know when you're ready."

Once the door is closed, I raise my voice at Beh. "You ready to tell us what's going on?" I ask.

"There might be cameras in here," Shabnam suddenly says.

"I don't care. I'm sick and tired of all these fucking secrets. You're going to tell us right now what's going on," I say.

The crying starts again. "I'm scared," Beh says.

"Don't be. Whatever it is, we can help you get through it," Shabnam tells her. She's a lot more patient than I'll ever be.

"I haven't been completely honest," Beh begins. "The night after Mâdar died, I snuck into their bedroom. I missed her and needed something of hers to help me sleep. I went into her closet, careful not to wake Padar."

She stops to wipe her tears. In a calmer state, she says, "I meant to grab a few of Mâdar's clothes and leave but then Padar woke up."

Again, Shabnam comforts Beh. She rubs her back.

"He was shuffling through his pills when he noticed me. He asked me why I was crying. I told him that I missed Mâdar," Beh says.

She cries again, this time for Padar. "He sat down in the closet with me. He held me and we both cried. That's when I just couldn't keep it in anymore. I told him I felt horrible for Mâdar's fall in the shower. He told me that he had guilt too."

I stop Beh from continuing any further, asking, "What did he tell you?"

"That he had pushed Mâdar and she'd fallen to the ground, having her first seizure. He said he could never forgive himself for not taking her to the hospital when it happened. He was afraid that the truth would come out and that he'd lose us," Beh says.

A tear runs down my cheek as I'm reminded of a bad memory. "Go on," I tell Beh.

"I then shared my guilt. Even though I was mad at him, I told him. I needed to tell someone."

"What did you tell him, Beh?" Shabnam asks.

"That I was going in there to tell her that Amir sexually assault-ed me . . . twice," she says, not able to look us in the eyes anymore.

Tears rush down my face. Shabnam buries her gasp in her hands.

"What?" I ask.

Shabnam throws herself in Beh's arms as I watch, still shaken up from all the pain.

"Why didn't you say something sooner?" Shabnam asks Beh.

"Every time I wanted to, something came up. I didn't want it to be about me when Mâdar was suffering so much," she says.

Again, anger takes over. "So Padar knew and he swept it under the rug?" I ask.

"No. He looked at me and said, 'I won't let that bachay sag get away with this.' He then got up and put his jacket on. When I asked him where he was going, he said, 'To make him pay.'"

"And then what happened?" I ask.

"I'm not too sure, but when he came back, he wasn't the same anymore," Beh says. "He came back soaked. I asked him what happened and why his clothes were so wet, and he said he went to visit Mâdar at her grave. He then took more sleeping pills and went straight to bed."

"So he didn't go to Kâkâ Farhad's house?" I ask.

"At first I thought he didn't. But then, the night of his death, when I found him in the attic, he was begging for my forgiveness. He kept saying, 'I'm sorry I can't do anything for you. They'll take Alif away from me,'" Beh says.

"Can you tell us why?" Shabnam asks.

"I don't know. He wouldn't tell me," Beh answers.

Anger takes me like a high. "I'm going to finish what Padar couldn't. That fat fucker is dead," I shout.

Shabnam runs to the door and stops me. "Wait," she says, "I want him dead, too, but this isn't the way to do it."

I grit my teeth. "Try stopping me!"

"You know I can," she says, threatening me with her blood. "Don't make me do it. Sit down and listen to what I have to say first."

After several attempts, Shabnam finally gets me to sit down.

"If you storm off now, Alice will want to know what's going on. The only way this'll work is if we tell her that we've agreed to have Kâkâ Farhad as our legal guardian, but only under one condition: that we first speak with him about a few things. If she asks what about, we'll say that we don't want him intimidating us to work at his market. Then, once we're there, we'll tell the truth about Amir, with Alice by our sides," Shabnam says.

Defensively, Beh asks, "And you think Amir is just going to admit it?"

"He doesn't have to, but at least Alice will be there to report it," Shabnam says.

Beh shakes her head. "This isn't going to work."

"It might, Beh. I think Shabnam's right," I say, to get things moving. The faster we're out of here, the faster I can put my fist through that fat fucker's face.

Shabnam comes close to Beh. With her hands on Beh's shoulders, she says, "I'd want nothing more than to go over there and drown Amir in my own blood. But we need to be smart about this."

Beh looks at me for approval. I nod.

"Fine," she whispers.

Before Shabnam opens the door, she says, "Let me do all of the talking."

Even though Alice agrees and willingly drives us to Kâkâ Farhad's house, I don't know if she's fully convinced — I'm too focused on my own anger.

I rest my hand on Beh's leg on the drive there. I wish she would've told me; I wish she didn't have to go through this alone. She's been through so much already — first, the guilt of blaming herself for Mâdar's tumour spreading, then watching Padar fall to his death and now, having to speak of the horrors done to her by Amir.

Alice rings the doorbell.

Khâla Wajma opens the door. One look at the white woman is all it takes for the waterworks to begin. "I'm so happy to see you all here."

As I scan the room for Amir, Kâkâ Farhad appears. Eyes red and swollen, he kisses our foreheads. When he tries to kiss mine, I push my way past him.

"Welcome. Please have a seat," he tells Alice.

We sit at the dining table. Tea and rout have already been prepared for us. Even the samovar and fancy teacups are out.

With a clenched jaw, I ask, "Where's Amir?"

"He's leading a *Quran* youth session at mosque," Khâla Wajma answers. For a woman who just lost her brother-in-law and a *dear* friend — khouârak jân, so she'd say — she's a lot smilier than usual.

She looks at Alice and says, "He really wanted to be here. He's really excited to have his cousins live with us. It's been a very difficult time for all of us."

I laugh. Shabnam's eyes dart at me.

Alice is also all smiles. Thinking that she's saved yet another family, she pulls several legal documents out of her briefcase. She says, "Before we get started, I believe the children wish to address a few concerns." She then looks at Shabnam, hoping that she'll be the one to speak.

"I need to be the one to say this." The words come out of my mouth. I let anger pour out of my eyes. "We will never live with you. This is the last time that you get to see any of us."

Alice looks confused. Kâkâ Farhad, however, does not. What, he'd thought that Beh would keep silent forever?

Khâla Wajma looks nervous as Beh begins to cry.

"Your son put his filthy hands on my sister, twice," I say.

The grand performance begins as Khâla Wajma hyperventilates and strikes her chest while Alice watches. Her eyes are now on us rather than her paperwork. She sits back and listens.

With a straight face, Kâkâ Farhad says, "I don't know what you're talking about."

I rise to strike him but Shabnam holds me back.

"How could you sit there and lie? You're supposed to be my kâkâ," Beh says, more heartbroken than ever.

Again, looking completely unaffected, he says, "I already told you that I don't know what you're talking about."

"Are you saying that you weren't aware?" Alice asks.

"I'm saying that none of this is true," Kâkâ Farhad says.

"You liar," Beh shouts. She then looks at Khâla Wajma and says, "And you knew all about it. You stood and watched!"

Another secret. Another lie.

Finally, Kâkâ Farhad looks affected. He looks at his wife, trying very hard to hide the hurt.

"What?" I ask Beh.

"Get them out of our house, Kareem," Khâla Wajma hollers. "What gives you the right to not only accuse my son of doing such a terrible thing but also make up lies about me?"

"Quiet. I'm warning you," Shabnam tells her. "Let my sister speak."

Beh can only look at me, Shabnam and Alice, for everyone in this room has betrayed her. "The second time Amir assaulted me, she found me crying in the bathroom. She tricked me into going to the basement with her so that she could scare me. She threatened me with the exact same words Amir did."

"What'd she say?" I ask, now crying.

Beh stutters. She can't bring herself to repeat those words. Eyes washed in sorrow, she looks down and says, "'Who's going to believe you? Amir, the *Quran* hâfez, or the fâyesha that showed her koss to Mr. Harvey?'"

"You fucking bitch!" I shout at the vile woman. This time, Kâkâ Farhad stops me. He holds me tightly by the arms and pushes me away.

Alice jumps from her seat. "I need you to step away and get your hands off of him," she tells him. She reaches for her cellphone and begins to dial.

"Wait," I tell her. I then look at the man who was once a brother to my padar and say, "You're going to tell us right now what happened the night Padar came here to confront the both of you."

"Why are you doing this, Alif? Do you want to end up like the children living next door to you?" Kâkâ Farhad asks.

With a painful lump in the back of my throat, I say, "We already are. Both of our parents are dead and we have no one to call family."

Finally, a crack in his voice. "Son, listen to me —"

"I'm not your fucking son! One last time, tell us what happened that night, that you had to send Yalda and Daoud over to scare Padar?" I ask.

Kâkâ Farhad keeps silent. So does his wretched wife.

I continue to push for answers. "You don't think I heard you arguing with Padar over the phone? Tell me or I'll call Yalda and Daoud myself."

Khâla Wajma finally speaks. She says, "I'll tell you why those two came over."

"Khafa sho!" Kâkâ Farhad tells her.

A tear runs down his cheek. He takes a deep breath and says,

"Your padar didn't want Yalda and Daoud visiting because he was afraid that they'd tell you . . . that . . . you aren't his real son."

My chest tightens. "What?" I ask.

Beh drops herself to the ground. Alice rushes to comfort her.

At first there's silence. Then, there's betrayal, hurt and every pain one could possibly think of slowly setting in. I think of all the times Mâdar and Padar had said "he's my son" and "he's our son" during their arguments.

"Farzana was pregnant with you before she met Kareem. No one knows the details; it was never talked about. I'm sorry you had to find out this way. Blood or not, he's your padar," he says, choking out the words right as he reaches for a cigarette from his back pocket and lights it.

"You son of a . . ." I say. I punch the wall and walk up to him. "You don't get to talk about blood."

"I'm so sorry. I never wanted you to find out," Kâkâ Farhad says. He tries to hold me but I step back.

"Padar came, I knew he did," Beh weeps. Her hands slightly shake. "And that's why he kept telling me he was afraid to lose Alif. Because you blackmailed him."

"It's your fault Padar's dead. You killed your own brother," I shout.

"Your padar died because he fell down a flight of stairs while heavily drugged. It was practically suicide," Kâkâ Farhad answers.

Shabnam's tight clasp again holds me back as I yell, "I'm going to fucking kill you."

I finally drop to the ground and cry. Beh and Shabnam fall down too, holding me in their embrace.

Kâkâ Farhad tries to come to me. He's crying. "Please, Alif jân, don't do this. Let's talk."

Shabnam stands. Blood, like arrows, shoots from her eyes. It stops a few inches away from Kâkâ Farhad's and Khâla Wajma's faces. "One more word and you'll both be sorry," she says.

Shaken up by Shabnam's blood, it takes Alice a moment to intervene. She says, "I've already asked you once, sir, to stay back. I'm going to have to call the police now. You understand I have a legal obligation to report that a child has been sexually assaulted."

Khâla Wajma becomes hysterical. "Harâmi," she yells at me. The word rips through my chest.

"Lower your voice," Alice says to her as she dials. "I'm going to need to know your son's whereabouts."

I tune out the voices, the screams and the cries as the police enter and take Khâla Wajma and Kâkâ Farhad in for questioning. I remain on the floor, vacant, for the next few hours as Shabnam and Beh continue to hold me. No one says anything, not even Alice.

We're all the monsters of the world: a sister that cries blood, a sister that bled by the hands of her family and then, there's me.

I don't even know my blood.

ACKNOWLEDGEMENTS

A heartfelt thank you to my publisher, Noelle Allen, for believing in *Monster Child*. To my wonderful and dedicated editor, Paul Vermeersch, thank you for believing in me. It has been an honour to work and learn from you. I would also like to thank Canisia Lubrin and Ashley Hisson for their invaluable editorial assistance. Finally, thank you to Jen Rawlinson and Brianna Wodabek.

Paul Matthew St. Pierre, you've devoted more time in helping me succeed academically, artistically and spiritually than anyone I know. I value your love and friendship. Thank you for being family to me.

To my partner in life, Joey, I love you. Thank you for supporting me and all of my dreams. None of this would be possible without your unconditional love and support. Thank you for pushing me to challenge myself.

To my little monsters, Malek and Matin, I wouldn't be here without either of you. Finally, I'd like to thank my greatest role models, my loving parents.

GLOSSARY

Note: The majority of the words and phrases found below originate from Dari, a dialect of Persian.

aberou: one's reputation. An expression to describe the good image others have of you.

alam: "flag" in Arabic. However, during the month of Moharram, the alam is a wooden pole with an emblem (usually a hand) to represent Abbas ibn Ali, the flag-bearer. This is a Shia Muslim tradition, and will be seen more often in regions where the Shia community is in the majority.

Allâhu Akbar, Allâhu Akbar. Bismillâh Arrahmân arrahim: in Arabic this means "Allah is great, Allah is great. In the name of Allah, the most beneficent and merciful."

andar: "step," as in stepsister, stepbrother, etc. . . . .

ăqâ: "mister," but Mâdar likes to use the term to convey the opposite, such as to mean an idiot.

ăsh: a noodle soup topped with a meat and lentil sauce, yogurt sauce and dried mint.

Ăshurâ: the word, which means "ten," is significant to Shia Muslims because it is the tenth day of the first lunar year, Moharram, which is the anniversary of the murder of Imam Hosein, the third Shia imam.

Astaghferullâh: an expression of shame, meaning "I ask God to pardon me."

azân: the call to Muslim prayer.

bâba jân: grandpa or father (bâba) dearest (jân). Alif, Shabnam and Beh use the term to mean grandpa.

Bacha hâye bâzingar: child-molesting men that force young boys to dance for their pleasure.

bachay sag: a swear word used by parents to curse their children.

Bâgh e Vahsh: zoo.

bandari: a common Afghani dance that is rhythmic and played in fast and slow tempos.

Band-e Amir: Afghanistan's first national park, this tourist attraction is known for its beautiful mountains and six lakes.

biâdar jân: "my dear brother."

bibi jân: grandma (bibi) dearest (jân).

Bismillâh: "in the name of Allah."

Bote Bâmiân: the Buddhas of Bâmiân were two statues carved into the cliffs of the Bâmiân Valley. The statues were destroyed in 2001 by the Taliban after they declared the statues were idols.

Châh e Zamzam: a holy well located in Mecca, Saudi Arabia. The well was miraculously created by Allah after Ibrahim's wife, Hajar, was left in a desert with her son, Ismail, who was crying from thirst.

châwa: a warm drink made from milk to help ease menstrual pain.

chenâq: a gambling game played with animal bones.

Darwâza ye kârwân wâ shod: "our home is not a hotel," which is said to mean that one's home is not an all-you-can-eat buffet.

du'â: a prayer.

esfand: incense burned to ward off the evil eye.

fânous: a lamp or light.

fâtiha: the name of the first chapter (surah) of the *Quran*. This chapter is recited often in funerals and in graveyards, but when Yalda and Daoud tell Alif, Beh and Shabnam that they wish to first give their fâtiha to Mâdar, it is used to express paying one's respect.

fâyesha: a derogatory term directed at women, meaning "slut."

ghaybat: gossip.

goudi parân: a kite.

hâfez: a Muslim that knows the *Quran* by heart.

halal: something that is permitted. The term is usually made in reference to food, especially meat, that is prepared according to Islamic practices.

haleem: a sticky textured dessert with shredded chicken, wheat, cinnamon and sugar.

harâm: something that is forbidden. The term is typically used in reference to food, especially meat, that is not prepared according to Islamic practices.

harâmi: "thief." But when Khâla Wajma calls Alif harâmi, she means bastard (i.e., child born out of wedlock).

Inshâllah: "God willing."

jân: "dearest."

jinn: referenced in the *Quran*. Created from a smokeless flame, these demonic beings were created at the same time as humans.

kâfir: non-Muslim / "foreign" countries.

kâkâ: uncle (father's brother only [as in Kâkâ Farhad] or when referring to another man older than you as a sign of respect).

kala pâcheh: a type of stew, which consists of sheep's head (kala) and hooves (pâcheh).

khafa sho: "shut up."

khâla: aunt (mother's sister only or when referring to another woman older than you as a sign of respect [as in referring to Wajma as khâla]).

khân: "ruler," but Mâdar likes to use the term to convey the opposite, such as to mean an idiot.

Khârej: "foreign" and Western societies.

Khodâ biamorz: although the words translate as "May God grant him/her forgiveness," this expression is used to convey "we are sorry for your loss."

khouârak jân: "dearest sister."

koss: a slang word for vagina, similar to "pussy."

lâjvard: lapis lazuli, a blue stone that's mined in northeast Afghanistan.

lirâ: Turkish currency.

litee: a warm drink made from flour to help ease menstrual pain.

mâdar: mother.

Maghrib: a mandatory salah (Islamic prayer) performed at sunset.

mâhicha: lamb shank.

mashk: water bag.

mehmouni: an invitation to one's home.

minbar: a pulpit in the mosque where a sheik delivers his sermons.

Moharram: a religious month specific to Shia Muslims that is dedicated to Imam Hosein, his family and his followers in the fight to keep Islam alive. It is also the first month of the Islamic calendar.

mohr: a chunk of soil or clay used for salat (Islamic prayers).

morda shouy khâna: a room, usually in a mosque, dedicated to washing deceased bodies.

Mubârak: "congratulations."

najis: impure.

Namâz e Jamâ'at: a collective prayer, where men and women are permitted to pray together, which is supposed to be rewarded more than individual prayer, but the women are to pray behind the men.

nana: an informal (and based on the tone, sometimes disrespectful) way of saying "mother."

nazars: amulets to ward off the evil eye.

nazr: during nazr, Muslims gather over dinner and Quranic recitations to celebrate something of importance.

niyyat: "intention." Niyyat is done before one performs their salat (Islamic prayers).

noha: a lament performed during the month of Moharram to commemorate Imam Hosein and those that passed in the Battle of Karbala.

Nowruz: the beginning of Spring and the Persian New Year.

padar: father.

padar nalât: colloquial form of "father cursed," used by parents toward their children.

pahlwâni: a form of wrestling common in Southeast Asia.

payran tomban: shirt and pants for men.

qâboli palaw: brown rice topped with chunks of lamb and fried raisins and carrot.

qara qol: hats made from lambskin.

qaymâq chây: a drink made from milk and tea and topped with a thick layer of milk skin.

qibla: the direction of the Kaaba (the sacred building at Mecca), to which Muslims turn at prayer.

qorma sabzi: spinach stew.

qurush: a silver coin.

robâb: a musical instrument originating from Afghanistan, similar to a lute.

rokou': a bowing down position in supplication.

rout: a bread that is sweet.

Rowza: religious poems that are sung in religious gatherings.

Salâm: a form of greeting exchanged between Muslims.

samovar: used to boil water for serving tea.

Sanâj: a Kabuli swear word meaning "jackass."

sekka: a gold coin.

shafâ: to cure.

Shia: a sect of Islam.

shikamba: tripe

shorwâ: a stew made with potatoes, beef and carrots.

simiân: a dish, usually eaten for breakfast, which consists of boiled rice noodles sprinkled with cardamom and sugar.

Sunni: a sect of Islam.

tasbeh: Islamic rosary (prayer beads).

tokhm-jangi: "egg fighting" consisting of two hard-boiled eggs. The players tap one another's eggs without breaking their own. The egg that breaks loses the game.

Towba: "Allah forbid."

Towzih ul Massâel: a book of Islamic laws by Ayatullâh Sistani, a spiritual leader to many Shia Muslims.

tushla: marbles.

wudhu: ablution or ceremonial washing done before performing prayers.

yakhni palaw: brown rice cooked in lamb broth and topped with chunks of lamb and fried raisins and carrots.

Zindagi sarâyetan bâsha: although this expression means "may you live a long life" and is said when paying one's respect for the deceased, the expression is used more to tell a grieving family may no other death be present in their family.

A mother of two, Rahela Nayebzadah holds a PhD in the Faculty of Education from the University of British Columbia. Currently, she is a schoolteacher. Her autobiographical novel, *Jeegareh Ma* (2012), was based on her family's migration to Canada from Afghanistan.